TRAILS OF RAGE

TRAILS OF RAGE

Todhunter Ballard

GUNSMOKE

First published in the UK by Prior Books

This hardback edition 2010
by BBC Audiobooks Ltd
by arrangement with
Golden West Literary Agency

ISBN 978 1 408 46251 5

British Library Cataloguing in Publication Data available.

Printed and bound in Great Britain by
CPI Antony Rowe, Chippenham and Eastbourne

Trails of Rage

CHAPTER ONE

Captain Jack Price, wearing heavy trousers, a sheep-lined coat and wide slouch hat instead of his blue uniform, braced himself on the jump seat behind the driver as the big red, gold-trimmed Overland coach rattled its way up the Platte.

A shotgun messenger rode beside the driver. Price was the only passenger, choosing to stay on top with the two men for what bits of information he might pick up from them.

The Indians had been especially active through the last months and no one who could avoid it traveled across the Plains these days. But Ben Holladay, to hold his mail contracts, had defiantly decreed that his coaches must move in spite of the evident determination of the Plains tribes to stop them.

Big Ben was no ordinary stage line owner. He had the ear of Congress. Better still, he was listened to by Abraham Lincoln, who knew well that it was imperative to keep traffic flowing east and west if the North ever hoped to win the struggle that was tearing the nation apart. It appeared a hopeless task with thousands of Cheyennes, Pawnees, Sioux and others bent on wiping out the white men and destroying the Overland, the hated invader of their hunting grounds.

Against that horde General Robert Mitchell had less than seven hundred troopers to guard twelve hundred miles of roadway and some six hundred stage stations. Business from Kansas through Denver and on to distant Salt Lake City had been brought to a near standstill. People refused travel in fear of their lives, for the lonely coaches were easy prey to bands of warriors.

A week earlier Captain Price, on leave recuperating from a shoulder wound, had been summoned to General Curtis' office. The General had seemed distraught.

"I've just been talking with Secretary Stanton, Captain. He has had word direct from the White House that the Overland Coach Line must be kept functioning at all costs. And we haven't anywhere near the numbers needed to patrol the Plains section."

Price made no answer, knowing that the General expected none. Curtis was given to thinking aloud. He went on.

"Now we have a new headache. Holladay claims to the President that it is not only Indians who are harassing him. He insists that bands of renegade Southerners are dressing like tribesmen to hit the stations. The President has sent word down that I am to find out whether or not this is so."

Still Price did not speak. Now Curtis looked at him keenly.

"What shape are you in? How's the shoulder?"

"Healing, sir, but slowly. I hope to be back in the lines before too long."

Curtis shook his head. "I need you right away, though not on the front, not fighting. You look well enough to ride the Overland as far as Salt Lake. Just surveillance. I have to know exactly what's going on out there. Frankly I don't trust Ben Holladay. If he saw any advantage to his stage line he'd have a thousand soldiers at every station. Still, if the raiders really are Southerners we'll have to react. It would be disastrous if they cut the country in two."

So Price had spent these last bitter days on the hard seat of the bouncing coach. The Concord, best vehicle of its kind made, had thoroughbraces that supposedly would ease the jar, but the neglected, frozen road was in such bad shape that nothing did any real good toward easing the pain that lanced through the shoulder at every jounce.

Parks, the driver, kept the six-horse team at a breakneck pace between the swing stations where the animals were replaced with fresh horses. Small, isolated places twelve to fifteen miles apart, their locations determined by the availability of water, they were built of logs or adobe with accommodations for a station keeper and a hostler only. Passengers stopped in them only under emergency.

Bracketing them every fifty or so miles, Ben Holladay, a lover of luxury, had established elaborate overnight hostels where a traveler could enjoy a comfortable bed and the best food to be found on the Plains. As the sole passenger since the stage had left Kearney, Price had had the choicest rooms and tables, and on this morning he looked forward to a two-day layover at Julesburg, just beyond the Colorado line, reported to be the finest station along the entire route.

But at the second swing station of the day they came on the first sign of Indian trouble. Topping a low hill, the driver swore with more feeling than his customary cursing out of the horses. Price lifted his chin out of the furry coat collar to look ahead. Across the plain where the next corral and little building should be there was only a black rubble of charred logs.

Ames, the shotgun messenger, came sharply alert, swiveling his head to study the wide, rolling country. Price too swept his eyes to the sides but could see no movement anywhere. Parks kept the team at a steady run until they reached the corral and pulled up there.

There was no living thing within sight. No horses in the pole enclosure. Two still, sprawled bodies lay beyond the rubble.

Price followed Ames, dropping down over the high front wheel, walking rapidly to the burned logs. There the messenger crouched, feeling among them, saying as he straightened,

"Cold. Day or more old."

They went on for a closer look at the bodies, then Ames turned back to the coach, Price at his heels. Parks, still on the seat controlling the team, called down.

"Bud and Jim? Scalped?"

Ames shook his head. "It's them, with the hair still on." His voice was bitter and suspicious.

Parks cursed viciously. "Johnny Rebs again, then. Damn them to hell. Get them inside here and let's get moving."

Ames made a slow turn, watching the distance, anxious.

"Ask me, we'd best turn us around and aim back the way we come while the team still has some run in it."

"Do that and we'd get us scalped for sure. By Big Ben. There's four mail sacks aboard that have to go through or else."

"Oh sure, sure. And what if there aren't any horses at the Big Spring station? If we get that far?"

The driver spat off to the side. "Then we go to Julesburg. What else? You two get those bodies loaded. I don't like it here."

Silently Captain Price went with the shotgun messenger to carry the hostler and station keeper, lay them inside the coach, then they climbed back to the top. He had expected to find such a scene as this somewhere along the line but the sight was nevertheless a shock, and the fact that the men had not been mutilated lent an ugly credence to the claim that white men were viciously masquerading as Indians. Still, it was not conclusive proof and his duty was to make sure. But there was a more immediate concern. He leaned forward toward the driver.

"This team, can it keep going without a rest? How far is Julesburg?"

"Twenty-one miles, with Big Spring in between. They can make it if they have to. Old Ben, he scours the world for the best animals money can buy. These can outrun any redskin pony alive when they're fresh and they can go all day if they're not pushed too hard. You just help keep a lookout, mister, and give a holler if company comes."

Price turned to face their rear while Ames and Parks scanned the road ahead and the hills around them, Parks nursing the big-chested, powerful animals, walking them up the grades, running them at a slower gait than the morning pace where the land dipped down, alternately walking and running them on the flats. It slowed their progress, created a sense of urgency to be out of the area, a rising expectation of attack. The pressure built in Price as the miles stretched out and he admired the control the driver showed, the exactness of his judgment that kept the team surprisingly fresh in spite of the work it had already done this day. Ben Holladay was noted for hiring all his drivers and guards personally, searching out abilities and characters to maintain the proud reputation of the Overland, and this man Parks must be a prime example of these lords of the road.

A grunt and a long, low growl from the two men brought Price swinging about to see ahead. They had come around a nose of hill and half a mile away the Big Spring station squatted on a knoll, a square adobe structure with a small hay barn and corral on the near side.

In this clear western air that foreshortened distances deceivingly Price made out that the pole enclosure was empty. But there were horses in the yard and figures standing there, still, as if transfixed.

Parks hauled in on the lines and immediately began to swing the team about. After the double run Price knew the tired animals could not outrace Indian ponies even with half-a-mile head start. He reached for his rifle and loosened the short gun in the civilian holster at his belt.

Part of this duty was the masquerade. General Curtis believed that the Captain could learn more from the

Overland employees if they were not aware of his military connection, that Ben Holladay would have ordered that only the story he was trying to sell in Washington be told, of Southerners plundering the relay points. The burned-out place they had passed could be a case in point, Parks's contention that white men were to blame. But his action now told plainly he expected something else here.

Ames, continuing to watch the figures, grunted again as the stage swung sideways of the road.

"Them's troops. I can see their hats."

Parks looked toward them. "But what color uniform?"

"Pull her down so I get a clear view." And when the coach had quit jolting across the ruts he said in relief, "Blue. It's all right."

Price let out the breath he had been holding and the driver veered back into the tracks, whipping the team to a last hard run as a bit of showmanship, pride in the company's prowess.

As they approached the blue began to stand out against the dun land and the white snow patches on the north side of the knoll, the army saddles bulked on the backs of the mounts. The soldiers were spotted about, still not moving, all facing the Overland vehicle as it rushed toward them. But before they reached the yard both Ames and Parks fell to a harsh cursing that Price did not know a reason for. Then the stage slowed to a walk, stopped, the six horses blowing gratefully after the last forced race. An officer without shoulder bars, a second lieutenant with only down on his young face, walked to the head of the team and called up.

"You'll get no animals here, driver."

He waved an arm at the adobe. Price saw then the door hanging askew, smoke blackened, and through the opening the burned wreckage of what had been the flat pole and brush roof. What at first sight had appeared a haven was a gutted empty shell of mud walls.

Parks said sourly, "I can see that for myself." The tone was eloquent of his small affection for the army. "How's Julesburg?"

"All right when we came through three days ago. We've been on scout. How is it east?"

"Clear between Fort Kearney and the last relay. That's gone. We brought the bodies. Not scalped. No Indians there."

The boy straightened, stiffened, said coldly, "Who else would it be?"

Parks spat, disdained to answer, anchored the lines and dropped over the wheel in an easy jump without touching it. Ames went off wordlessly on his side and as Price followed they pulled open the coach doors, flapped their hands at the interior and turned away, went back to the boot for canteens, took them to the mud wall and squatted there in the warmth of the sun for the water they had passed up at the station behind.

Price saw no bodies in the yard but did hear the scrape of shovels somewhere behind the little building and started around it to see the condition of whoever had been caught and killed here.

Against the side wall, also in the sun, firewood was stacked, not molested by the raiders. Captain Price stopped in mid-stride. A woman huddled on the pile, one elbow on her knee, her head lowered into a hand that covered her face, a tangle of long very light hair stringing down her back and forward across her shoulders.

An exclamation of surprise burst from him. She lifted her head, looked toward him with dazed eyes that he thought did not focus on him. His surprise changed to shock. Even in this disheveled condition he recognized Sue Steelman, General Steelman's pretty daughter.

CHAPTER TWO

"Sue. Great God." Price's long legs stretched his stride.

The girl stared for a second longer then lifted to her feet and ran, coming into his arms as if coming home.

"Jack. Jack Price."

The call was high, near hysteria and a flood of tears sprang from her eyes, made rivulets through the dust and dirt streaks on her cheeks. The glove silk traveling dress was smudged and stained. Her hands trembled, clawing at his chest.

"Oh, Jack, Jack, Jack. How awful."

The young Lieutenant had heard Price's shout and the girl's wailing voice and came at a run, bound on protecting her if there was new danger here. He saw the embrace with a flush of jealousy, stopping five feet away. His voice was rough.

"Ma'am, you know this . . . this . . . ?"

The blond head nodded against Price's heavy coat. The words came muffled. "I surely do, and oh what a relief to see him here. Lieutenant Price. I knew him at the Point."

This was not the moment to correct the rank. He had not seen her since he had earned his battlefield promotion. The disclosure of his identity annoyed him, but at least it was a fellow army man who heard it and it could be stopped at this point, spread no further. On top of jealousy the young officer was suspicious.

"Lieutenant? What are you doing out of uniform?"

To stop a grilling, Price's tone was short. "Captain. Do not ask questions, Lieutenant. I am on detached duty. It is not to be mentioned by either of you. Now, Sue, what in the world are you doing here?"

The girl had leaned back, for the first time aware of the civilian clothes. She pulled away as though instinctively shying from the nonmilitary fabrics. The Lieutenant's flush had deepened with affront and his lips formed a protest before he thought better of it and choked it off. Sue Steelman looked from one to the other, her brows raised.

"Captain now? That's good to hear, Jack, and I won't say a word. Me? I'm on my way to join Aunt Mae in Denver because Dad was ordered to report to Grant and he felt I would be safer out of wartime Washington. Two days ago the stage stopped here to change horses. It was a chance to visit the, well, outhouse. I was there when I heard screeching and shots, terrifying noises. I stayed there in a fright, thinking I'd be found any minute, but they didn't look in there. A long time later it got quiet outside but I didn't move until after dark." She spread both hands against her cheeks and the deep blue eyes darkened with memory, the voice thinned to a shrill. "When I did creep out the station roof was still burning. The flames . . . the light . . . everybody was dead." The eyes squeezed shut and the tone shrilled higher. "The two men at the station. The driver and shotgun messenger. My escort, Lieutenant Brown. The three other passengers. Their heads all looked red. Red. I thought it was firelight until morning. Then I saw." She drew a long, ragged breath, rocked her head hard to get rid of the picture and went on in a shaken rush. "The stage was gone and all the horses." She sagged against Price again.

He put an arm around her, half carried her back to the woodpile and lowered her onto it, saying very quietly, "Did you look out? Did you see the attackers?"

"One at the beginning, through the crescent in the door. He had a hatchet and a feather in his headband. Almost naked. His face was painted but he wasn't as dark as I thought Indians were. Oh, how ugly he was, running after a man."

Across her blond head the young Lieutenant's eyes challenged Price's hotly. Plainly he too had heard the brutal rumors of Southerners being responsible for these depredations and was having second thoughts about the stage driver's flat statement, "No Indians there." The Captain used one strong hand against the girl's bent neck in a gesture of comfort, but since she was safe and unhurt his attention went to the other man.

"How long have you been at Big Spring, Lieutenant?"

The slender body was rigid with tension. Price read the hostility and continued suspicion of this purported officer who was riding the coach out of uniform, and the answer was clipped.

"Two hours. We rode in, found the station wrecked and presumed everyone was killed. We were astounded to see Miss Steelman sitting here."

The girl's head lifted. "Like a miracle, their coming. I'd

been here two days. Without food. I didn't know what to do or when another stage would come. I didn't dare walk . . . out there . . ." Her eyes were not on Price but on the young officer, and as she talked of their arrival a look of outright adoration replaced the terror that had been behind them. She straightened, found an incredible smile. "Then Lieutenant Hamilton was here and it was all right. He had coffee and bacon made for me, and nothing ever tasted so good."

Captain Jack Price understood the change in her only too well. It turned a knife in him, made him unnecessarily rough with the youngster.

"Where are you stationed, Lieutenant?"

"Fort Sedgwick. Few miles below Julesburg." At the chill in Price's eyes he reluctantly added, "Sir."

"What are you doing up here?"

"Chasing Indians of course. Since the massacre they're out everywhere."

At Sand Creek, so few days before. Price had only heard of it at Kearney and had been appalled. From the Cheyenne reservation at the junction of Sand Creek and the Arkansas bands of braves had harassed the country all through the last summer but with the onset of winter had drifted back to be fed by the very army they had been attacking. That had become an increasingly sore point among the settlers, prospectors, and trappers who had lost family and friends. The protests had reached the press and there was a howl that something be done.

Under that pressure Colonel Chivington was sent to Fort Lyon, close to the reservation. He might have arrested the leaders of the raiding parties and quieted the storm. Instead he marched to the village, found most of the men off hunting but attacked anyway, wiping it out. Most of those slaughtered were women and children.

Even the whites who had cried for action were horrified and at Kearney there was a rumor that the tribes were holding a war council, forgetting their differences to band together, but the consensus was that it was much too soon to expect any retaliatory raids.

Price said, "What kind of exaggeration is that from an officer, that they are out everywhere?"

The boy insisted stubbornly, "No exaggeration, sir. For a hundred miles around Sand Creek the ranches have been burned. Stages and stations hit. Towns deserted. Even in Denver there's a curfew, every able-bodied man turned out to drill."

Price reached for breath to control himself, for if what the Lieutenant said was true there was no cause to ride him.

He said more easily, "That's all south of here, Hamilton. Anything north to take you that way?"

"Reason to think so, sir." There was less antagonism in the voice than something near awe. "We picked up the tracks of a big war party above Julesburg. We followed it for two days, then cut back to see what shapes the stations were in. We found this." His upturned hand made a slow sweep of the desolation. "I suggest, sir, that as soon as the burials are finished we move for town. The day's getting on."

Price saw the worry tighten the face and forced a smile.

"I won't pull rank on you here, Lieutenant. It's your command. Get ahead with it."

In relief Hamilton snapped a salute, wheeled away, striding to the rear of the 'dobe to check the progress there. Price trailed him, found a common grave had been dug and the eight scalped bodies laid in it. Troopers were just bringing the hostler and driver from the coach, around the far side of the building where Sue Steelman need not see them, followed by Parks and Ames. But the General's daughter was not to be denied a part, or perhaps did not want to be left alone, edging around behind the 'dobe to where the men were.

The last two bodies were laid with little ceremony beside the others as the Lieutenant called his order. "Lynch, on the double, have that trench filled in and tamped good."

A big, heavily built sergeant with a craggy face swept a thick arm, waving in the diggers resting on the shovels. They wasted no time throwing sandy soil into the upturned faces, the sightless eyes and mouths frozen open in soundless screams. The girl had not looked into the trench, hanging back against the wall, but when the grave was tamped flat and Hamilton turned abruptly toward the horses she ran to him, catching his arm, sounding shocked.

"Lieutenant. Not even a prayer for their souls?"

The young man flushed, looking about somewhat wildly, Price thought, wanting to have his detail mounted and on the Julesburg road. Ames, the shotgun messenger, coughed and stepped forward.

"My pa was a preacher, soldier. I know the words and a few can't hurt any."

Hamilton bit his lip, threw a sidelong glance at the blonde and nodded curtly. "The time . . . very well. Make it brief."

So the small troop stood at attention for ten minutes while a man with a gun across his arm consigned the good dead brethren to the arms of the Lord.

The amen was still resonant on the air when the Lieutenant took the girl's arm firmly, piloted her to the stage and handed her inside, immediately afterward mounting his men.

Price rode the coach with Sue Steelman below the driver and shotgun messenger and noted that Parks used his team more impatiently again. Seventeen troopers led by Hamilton and Sergeant Lynch trotted ahead as escort, far enough in the lead that the cold Plains wind took their dust off to the side so the team animals did not choke on it.

Sue Steelman sat rigid, peering out through the windows on one side and then the other, looking for Indians. Jack Price tried to set an example of relaxation, resting his big knuckled hands on his knees, his spine against the seat back, and surreptitiously watched the girl.

As the years had passed he had lost the hope of seeing her again and had thought of her less and less. Along with half the plebes in his class he had been in love with her even though he recognized her as a flirt who used men to feed her vanity. Small, fine boned, her fair hair woven with strands of gold when the sun touched it, she had had a strong appeal which he felt again now and resolutely put away from him. Unlike some of his classmen who came from wealthy families, he had come from a New England mill town where his father was still a struggling lawyer. He had known from the beginning that once he was through the Academy he would have only his army pay to live on, and known even then that no girl such as Sue Steelman would be content with the poverty of a second lieutenant's wife. Yet he had dreamed. A long breath, almost an audible whistle escaped him.

She turned her head from the window and surprised his attention upon her, flushed prettily and asked quickly, "What are you thinking, Jack?"

He evaded. "Being amazed at the coincidence of our both being here so far from where we might expect to meet. You aren't married?"

The blue eyes slanted up at him. "Not yet."

"But you have him picked out?"

She appeared to consider seriously before she answered, then, "I'm not sure. He's English, in their embassy. I'm not certain I would like England; they say it's a cold, damp, dreary country."

He was nonplused. The inference that she would marry or not marry a man hinging on a matter of climate was beyond him. He retreated to silence. Even as a youngster who had felt the pull of sexuality he had seen that she was spoiled and selfish, but in his dream, if he could marry her he could change her more to his liking. A moment ago he had hoped that by drawing her out in conversation he could relieve her tension but he wanted no more jolts like this.

And in her apprehension she let the short flow of talk dry up. Time dragged, both of them wrapped in cocoons of memories, feeling constraint yet extremely conscious of each other as the swaying coach threw them against each other again and again.

The yell came sudden, shocking from the top of the coach. Under the whip the jaded team lunged to a near runaway gallop. Snapping a look through the window, Price saw they were passing the mouth of a draw. Indians in a ragged line were driving down that toward the stage.

Sue Steelman screamed, holding the piercing sound that covered Price's sharp order to get down on the floor. When she did not obey he caught her shoulder roughly and forced her between the seats, reaching for his rifle with his other hand. He opened the door, twisted out to the step, straightened to claw at the hand rail above and scrabble to the rocking roof, slipping once but catching himself, throwing himself onto the top between the driver and the jump seat.

He had a glimpse of Parks, straining forward, shouting, flailing his whip, of Ames using a rifle that reached farther than his Greening. Rising to look ahead, he saw the escort, the boy Lieutenant wheeling them, the arm above his head sweeping forward. At first Price thought he was signaling a charge at the Indians, then as if he changed his mind Hamilton strung the troopers out in a skirmish line, spread them abreast of the racing coach between it and the on-coming red men as a screen.

Already in sight were more Indians than there were soldiers and men on the stage, and still they streamed down the coulee, snow and dust boiling up from pony hoofs to lay about like rising fog.

The Captain had not been conscious of how the sky had lowered, of the thick blue-black clouds that rolled over the whole scape promising storm. In an aftervision like a photograph at the back of his eyes he recalled the picture ahead to the west, a huddle of blocky buildings perhaps a mile away, black, low-lying shapes against the gloom and behind them, silhouetting them for a second, one slender, brilliant shaft as red as blood that had found a rift, the last flare from the setting sun. That would be Julesburg, with a population to fight off the attack. If they could make it.

Choosing ponies as targets easier to hit than the riders he began firing over the heads of the troopers, shooting only when the coach tilted up on that side. Ames had jumped over both the front and second seats and lay flat on the roof, picking off the Indian horses methodically.

Parks continued to lash the team but Price sensed they were faltering. Only the wild yipping cries of the Indians, designed to terrorize an enemy, gave the animals the desperation to press on.

Ponies were falling. But so were troopers and their horses. And the tribesmen were gaining. Price saw one blue figure fall as the mount pitched forward, roll to one knee to continue fighting. He was overrun by a group of braves, shot three off their ponies before one wheeled beside him and drove a lance through his upper body.

Hamilton's thinning line closed up but the ranks of Indians continued to increase and the detail could not cover the whole advance. Many red riders were getting near enough to use their bows. Arrows filled the air, stabbing into the boot of the stage.

With a sharp shout the shotgun messenger suddenly sprang up, twisting, grabbing at the back of his shoulder. Price saw the winged arrow deeply bedded there before the stage jolted and threw Ames off. The rear wheel jounced high, rolling over him.

The driver Parks was next. He yelled and Price saw the wicked shaft quiver in his back. Jumping to the front seat, the Captain saw blood spill from the contorted mouth, making a gurgle of the man's last words. "Take over."

Jack Price dropped his rifle, grabbed the reins from the dying hands and fought the team. It was all but out of control. There was no time now to help with his gun or even to watch the running fight. All his attention was needed to keep the animals in the roadway.

He sensed the first straggling buildings of Julesburg as they careened into the town. But he saw no one. Nor was there any firing from the doors or windows of the entire three block length of the street. And the sounds of guns now behind the stage were pitifully few, the Indian cries much louder, closer.

There was wind now, gusts that blew dry powder snow and dust across the ruts. He saw the station, the big pole corral on the near side, saw the gate of that swung open, yanked the team leaders that way, rocketed through. He had a passing glimpse of a female figure running, pulling the gate wider. Then he was beyond her, sawing on the reins to bring the panicked team down before it should crash headlong into the log building dead ahead.

Price had a swift impression of logs more than a foot through, of narrow windows almost at head height to a standing man, more nearly gun slits than conventional apertures, Ben Holladay's insurance against attack. He dragged at the rein to wheel the team aside. They turned in time but barely, the hub of the rear wheel screeching along the building side. They quit then and stood trembling, heaving.

Jack Price dropped the reins, snatched up his rifle and jumped to the ground. Pulling the coach door open, he hauled out Sue Steelman, slung her across his shoulder and raced for the open door of the station. It let him into a long barroom where a fire burned in a fireplace at the far end and tables were spotted between. He bent, unceremoniously dumped the girl into the closest chair and in the same motion whirled to run back outside.

A swift scanning of the corral showed him only the big Sergeant Lynch and two troopers, the remnant of the detail, flung out of their saddles and kneeling against the lowest pole, shooting through the bars toward Indians now circling out of range of the rifles, shaking their bows, howling. Beside the soldiers a thick-set middle-aged man held a gun leveled but did not fire, conserving ammunition. The woman who had opened the gate had just closed it, fastened it and turned toward the men.

She was tall, young, black haired, her stride easy, showing her in control, not excited, passing Price to go into the building.

Heading toward the four men, Price saw the sergeant turn his head, say something to the civilian, saw the man shrug and move off to open the gate again. Lynch was on his feet jogging to the spent team. He took the near lead animal by its nostrils, forced it to face the gate. The others moved with it as they were trained. Lynch led them near the opening, then with an abrupt shout, slapping his gun against the rump, firing it close to the horse's ear he stampeded the whole team outside.

"That'll keep the red devils interested for a while."

The civilian slammed the gate shut again, dashed for the house and Lynch sent a shrill whistle to the two troopers, waved them with him and they all followed the man. Inside he dropped a heavy bar across the door, then mopped his face with a bandanna.

"Close one, that."

Sergeant Lynch and his troopers went immediately to the slit windows, looking out toward the wheeling Indians who yipped and howled in new anticipation. Price chose a fourth slit, knocked out the glass with the muzzle of his rifle and shoved the snout through, shivering involuntarily as the heat from the fire made its impact on his cold body. He had been too busy to notice it before but snow was now whirling through the wind outside, creating a haziness between him and the red warriors beyond the corral. They were cautiously moving closer. With the whites bottled up inside the younger braves were impatient for a slaughter.

Without turning Lynch shouted across his shoulder, "Ryan, where the hell is everybody? Your hostlers, your cook, waitresses. This town looks dead empty."

"It is," the man called back from the thick door, where he was shoving a heavy bar into brackets. "Warning came yesterday an attack was due and all Julesburg lit for Fort Ryan like a pack of mangy coyotes. Everybody but my daughter and me."

Price marked the man then as the keeper of this station. "Why did you stay?"

Ryan snorted loudly. "Hell, man, Ann and I been through so many Indian scares we can't count them. At every station we've had. If we'd run whenever somebody yelled, Ben Holladay would have fired me long ago. But I didn't expect a thousand 'skins to come down on me. Annie, go rustle some coffee and grub for us."

CHAPTER THREE

Ryan's tone held only scorn without a hint of fear, and
the girl turned without hurry toward the kitchen. To Price
their behavior was more than strange. The station man-
ager had moved to a slit and begun a methodical firing,
joining the soldiers already shooting. But the numbers outside foretold the certainty of how this siege must end.
Price doubted that there was sufficient ammunition in the
building to provide one bullet for each red man even
though every shot went true.

He drew his short gun, left his window and went to the
chair where Sue Steelman still huddled, and folded the
gun into her hand, bending to kiss her forehead.

"You're a general's daughter," he told her. "Remember
that when they come. Take your own life. It will be easier
for you than capture."

He turned back before emotion should betray him but
Ryan stopped him as he passed, speaking low.

"No need for that. Not yet anyway. Just scare her
worse."

The Captain bridled at the illogic of the man, said
curtly, "There is need. We are all going to lose our hair
and you know it."

Ryan was cocky. "Ain't lost it yet, mister."

"You will. It's only a matter of time."

Ryan fired and over his head Price saw a brave knocked off his horse before the man spoke again.

"Time's on our side."

"Against that force? Do you know something you haven't told us?"

"Don't need to tell somebody who knows this country. Blizzard starting. Night coming fast."

Price moved away to cover his window again, shooting as targets came within range, in some degree satisfied to see that between the five of them they were accounting for enough Indians to stall the concerted rush, puzzled now at what Ryan's words meant. He raised his voice to reach him.

"What special virtues are there in those prospects? Snow and darkness will only give them cover to move in under when we can't see them."

"Nope, stranger, because they're too superstitious to fight at night. Afraid if they're killed then their Great Spirit can't find them and they'll wander in limbo for-ever. . . . Pay attention now, here comes a rush."

The only sounds in the room then were the blond girl's quiet wailing and the explosions of rifle fire. The snow was thickening, swirling in clouds across the yard. Indian figures materialized out of it, riding by, throwing firebrands toward the roof, shooting arrows in a rain against the logs, arrows the rising rage of wind deflected and threw into the air. Men and ponies sprawled on the ground changed from dark figures in the failing light to white mounds, formless and still. But others kept coming who were not hit. The troopers and Ryan would fight as long as they were alive, but Price was convinced that would not be for long. He called to Ryan.

"In this wind that roof will be an inferno in no time, drive us out. How dark does it have to be to stop these people?"

"Darker than now, but forget the roof. Soon as I heard about the scare I started hauling water. It's soaked clear through by now. Quit stewing and keep them back. Hey, you, miss," his voice slammed hard at Sue Steelman. "There's a job you can do. Over behind the bar there's a stash of ammunition. Fetch it and pass it around."

The girl stood up, obeying like an automaton. She looked blankly at the heavy gun in her hand as though it were a snake ready to strike, laid it gingerly on the chair and went back of the bar. When Price saw her again the front of her skirt was gathered into a pouch and weighted with cartridge boxes. She took them from window to window where the men caught out handfuls, reaching Price last. He was too busy to reach for them, firing rapidly as four Indians raced by lying low along the off side of their ponies, shooting the animals from under them, then hitting the men as they scrabbled for their feet.

He heard the clatter as the remaining boxes were dumped to the floor, heard Sue's high scream as she looked through the window across his shoulder and glanced around, thinking an arrow he had not seen had come through and struck her. But her hands were clapped over her face, she turned, ran to her chair, dropped into it on top of the gun and threw the skirt up over her head.

When he looked back at the yard he saw six or seven Indians hit by the others go down. Because of the growing dark and the blinding snow he could not be sure of numbers. Then the attack broke off, the sortie retreated and nothing out there moved except one wounded pony thrashing to get up.

There was movement beside him. Ann Ryan was there putting down a chair with a mug of coffee and a plate of sandwiches on the seat, giving him an encouraging smile as she straightened. Hunger came suddenly. Because of the burned-out swing stations he had had nothing to eat since morning.

He swallowed coffee, finished a sandwich in two bites, found the other men already hurriedly swallowing the food. Ann was setting a plate and mug on the table where Sue Steelman sat, then firmly tugged the skirt down over her knees. He had a glimpse of Sue's eyes coming up, smoky with fear, onto the calm face of the other girl.

There was sharp contrast there. Sue with her fragile, Dresden doll beauty, too terrorized for further movement. Ann Ryan, her dark hair parted in the middle, drawn to a lush coil at the nape of her neck, lifting the coffee mug and holding it against Sue's rigid lips, all but forcing her to drink, saying something Price could not hear. He marveled at her composure in the face of certain death.

Sergeant Lynch left his window to walk close to Price and say in a low rumble that carried only inches, "No time to tell you before, sir. When Lieutenant Hamilton went down and I tried to help him he said I couldn't. Told me you're a captain on detached duty from the East. Welcome to Colorado, sir." There was strong uneasiness in his next words. "You want to take command here?"

Price lifted one corner of his wide mouth, touched the Sergeant's sleeve in a gesture to relax him. "I do not. I wouldn't know what to do in this situation. If you do, go ahead."

Lynch tried to conceal his sigh of relief. "Well, looks like their show's over for tonight. Gives us time."

Looking through the window, Price found the driving snow so thick now he could see only a couple of yards. Indians could be directly below, against the wall, and he would not know it.

"I hope you're right, Sergeant." His tone doubted the man.

"I am, Captain." Lynch spoke with confidence but not braggadocio. "I've been on this duty four years and never knew the hostiles to move against us in the dark. Besides, we've got one hell of a blizzard going for us and those Indians aren't exactly dressed for it. There'll be squaws behind them by now setting up lodges, building fires. They'll hole in tonight and have another go at this station in the morning. They won't hurry, that many of them. They know the army hasn't men enough within a hundred miles to tackle them. We'll be all right."

Price arched his brows in disbelief. "All right through the night, you mean."

"Just plain all right. We'll start making ready now to walk out to Fort Sedgwick. It's only a few miles south and we should make it in a couple of hours."

For the first time since they had arrived at Julesburg the Captain felt the lift of hope. They had a chance.

"What about your horses?"

Lynch shook his head. "If there are any left alive or not run off they'd be too risky. Harness noise or a blow or whinny would give us away."

"Could you find the way through the storm?"

The Sergeant nodded with a half grin. "Sure. Go downhill to the river and follow it. Fort's on the other side but there's ice to cross on." He raised his voice to the room, announced the plan and told them to prepare themselves.

The troopers stuffed their pockets with shell boxes. Ryan went for rope as Lynch directed. Ann Ryan, eying Sue Steelman's inadequate traveling clothes, disappeared and returned with a buffalo robe that she wrapped around the blonde's shoulders and pinned at the neck, then she shrugged into her own sheep-lined greatcoat and held another for her father when he brought two long coils of rawhide lariat.

Lynch had collected the mugs, added more coffee, brought a bottle from the bar and laced each drink heavily with whiskey for internal warmth. They all gathered, silent, at the table. The Sergeant strung one rope through one trooper's belt and tied it, leaving a long end trailing. The other end he threaded through Ryan's belt, drew it up to separate the men by some five feet, and another five feet back wrapped it around Ann Ryan's waist, cinching in the coat with a knot. Ann had Sue on her feet, took the lariat from Lynch to fasten the girl in the next place, then at Lynch's gesture passed the remaining line to Price. The

Captain linked himself to the others and shoved his short gun into his holster.

Lynch and the second trooper still stood free, the Sergeant beckoning everyone through the bar into the kitchen, where a lamp burned low.

"Leave the bar light burning," he ordered generally. "Wait here for us. Kelly, kill that lamp. First hitch yourself to this other line, then we'll have a look around outside."

When the second trooper had blown down the lamp chimney inky blackness blotted out the room. Price heard their boots cross the floor, heard the grate of a bar being removed from the rear door, the increased howl of wind and felt the icy blast as flying snow rushed in against his face when the door was briefly opened. It was closed and the trooper with them braced his back against it, holding it against the wind.

They waited. No one spoke. The storm made the only sounds. The two men outside were gone too long to suit Price. Frowning, he wondered if they had lost contact with the building, were blundering blindly through the black night, or had been caught by Indians guarding this exit. He felt his way past the girls and Ryan to the door where the trooper stood, straining to hear through the thick planks. More time passed. Then abruptly the trooper lunged forward, stumbled into Price and both nearly fell. The door was shoved open. There was a confusion of movement, and Lynch's low voice.

"Henley, hand us your rope end."

Price sensed that the Sergeant was tying the man who had gone with him and himself onto the string of people.

"Where you been all this while?" Ryan growled. "I figured you was lost for sure."

Mike Lynch chuckled. "Not likely. Kelly and I had the rope between us. He stayed put against the walls while I made a sweep around the station looking for a sentry."

Ryan grunted. "You didn't think any of that kind would stand out in this storm, did you?"

"Yep. And he was there. He won't bother us now. His throat's cut."

Price pictured the blizzard. With that and the night Lynch could not have seen a hand held before his eyes. He said in wonder, "How could you locate him?"

"Smelled him." The Sergeant sounded smug. "If you'd ever been downwind of an Indian winter camp you'd savvy." He raised his voice a little to be sure they all heard. "Time to move out now. Don't anybody make a noise. There's probably no savages close enough to hear but I don't want to take chances. I'll lead with Kelly behind me. Wait for the line to tighten, then walk as close as you can to the pace of those in front of you. Don't crowd up on them or bump into them, and try not to fall. We could lose our bearings trying to get somebody up."

The storm lashed at them through the open door. Over its noise Price could not hear footsteps but after a moment the rope between himself and Sue Steelman pulled taut and he moved with it. The pace was cautious, all of them feeling their way through the doorway, down the single step to the frozen ground. At the rear end of the train Price kept the line tight to give what support he could to Sue.

He felt a suffocation, a sense of walking through a

feather quilt except that the wind-driven snow pellets stung against his skin. He could see nothing at all, but his left hand scraped on the peeled-log wall as Lynch took them along it for guidance before leaving it to make for the river. As yet he felt no dropping grade under his feet. There would probably be some distance to cover on the flat where Lynch could make a turn without knowing it, lead them in a blind circle, lose them, walk them onto the Indians even.

The snow was a foot deep and deepening but Lynch and the men ahead were breaking track that the girls could manage and as Price followed he found the footing somewhat slippery but not too bad.

The Sergeant's soft call reached back to him. "Hill turns down now. Take it sideways like stairs and mind your step. Not far to the river now."

Price moved up until he could catch Sue Steelman's hand to steady her on the decline. Her nails clawed into his palm and her arm shook like palsy with cold and fright. Then the wind abated a little, the flying snow was less dense. Something made Sue gasp, then the branch of a tree she had run into bent and snapped back, slapping against Price's stomach. He breathed in relief. There would be a belt of trees along the riverbank such as he had seen along the watercourses of the Prairie, most of them less than an eighth of a mile thick. The letup of the wind was welcome.

"We go through some cottonwoods here." Lynch's voice barely reached the back of the train. "Close up so you don't come a cropper on one. When we get through there's a bank, maybe six, seven feet high we'll have to slide down."

Engulfed in the trees, they would be harder to locate than on the open plain. Jack Price's back muscles had been bunched, tight with apprehension as he waited for an arrow or a hatchet. The strong wind still brought the stench of the Indian camp as if it were only yards behind them, the smoke of buffalo chip fires in the lodges where he hoped they were all waiting out the night. This bloody frontier was too new to him to put full faith into what others claimed as fact. Of only one fact was he certain. The more than a thousand men who had chased them, killed so many troopers, besieged the station were not Southern rebels. They were genuine tribesmen, the first the Captain had seen, and he fervently hoped the last he would see.

There was one comforting thought. Snow blowing across the ground would have already filled the trench and smoothed over their tracks outbound from the station for much of the quarter mile they must have come.

CHAPTER FOUR

They joined hands to help each other down the steep riverbank, but as Price set one foot over the edge Sue Steelman's feet skidded out from under her. She crashed into Ann Ryan and in a domino spill all those ahead fell and Price was yanked down on top of the pile.

At the bottom standing up again became a problem. The wind had whipped the ice clear of snow. The hard, smooth surface was treacherous. In the scramble to untangle themselves Price backed away on his buttocks, dragging Sue free by the line between them, surprised that their combined weight crashing down together had not broken through into the water. He had a wayward thought that brought an unexpected chuckle rumbling in his throat.

In the lake country of his native East the woodsmen had spent the deep winter days with horse and sleigh cutting ice in cubes sometimes three feet deep to be hauled ashore and packed in sawdust for supplies that would last through the summer. Price had asked old Jake Unger once how thick ice needed to be to support a load. One inch would hold a man, Jake said. Two would carry a man and a horse. Three, a man, a horse and a wagon. "Four inches will take a man, a horse, a loaded wagon *but keep moving.*"

The memory lightened his mood. He set his feet, straightened, careful of his balance, and bent, reaching for the blond girl. In the black dark he bumped heads with Ann Ryan, also trying to help Sue, and they all fell again.

He was startled by a low giggle from the station keeper's daughter and his own chuckle broke out in muted laughter, then both choked off the small sounds. But his tension was gone and another lift of admiration for Ann Ryan warmed him through.

It took time and much care to get the whole party up and moving again, step by mincing step across to the eastern shore, buffeted by the wind that nearly blew them down again and again. It was easier at the far bank where there was brush on the slope to pull themselves on by. Then they were in trees again with the gale broken. Price heard Sue's ragged, gasping, moaning breaths and called softly to Lynch.

"Sergeant, the girls need a rest. What do you think?"

"Should be all right now," the answer came. "But ten minutes only. No telling how long this snow will last to cover us."

Price felt for the girl ahead, eased her down and stretched himself full length on the snow, tired out himself from the day's ordeal. He closed his eyes and drifted into a doze, then sharply forced himself awake. Sleepiness was the first warning that the body was close to freezing. He sat up quickly, crawling to Sue Steelman, calling her name harshly.

She sounded drowsy, far away. "Mmmm?"

He caught her arm through the buffalo robe, shook her,

intentionally rough. "Don't go to sleep. Get up. Stamp your feet. Ann, are you awake?"

"I am," she said.

Sue protested, "But I'm so tired, so tired."

Price lifted the blonde, held her on her feet with one arm around her, slapped her cheeks, talking. "Fight it, Sue, or you'll freeze. Swing your arms. Stamp. Get your blood moving."

Sergeant Lynch cut short the rest stop as too dangerous a temptation, got everyone up and they went on, fumbling through the belt of cottonwoods. Within their shelter the snow fell much less hard but the blackness was intense. Price felt akin to a mole burrowing blindly through the ground.

Without warning there was a sudden change. They had passed the trees, were again on the lumpy grass clumps that mounded the deep snow. The blizzard was gone, the white falling blanket stopped altogether. One moment Price could see nothing at all. The next he made out the figures strung along the lifeline, the heads and backs thickened with snow.

There was an opalescence to the air. Looking up, he was astonished to see the sky now freckled with its million stars, distant, cold, their brilliance magnified. Had he known more about the high country he would not have been so taken aback. Many of the heaviest storms there were local to small areas. A man could ride into and out of a torrent within minutes. Turning his eyes west, he saw the pale shapes of snow-covered peaks glowing under the starlight. His reaction was that he had broken out of a dungeon. He breathed the cleaned, wine air with deep relish.

With Julesburg across the river and behind the screen of trees he could not see it. The smell of Indian fires had faded. He could, Price thought, forget the savages and concentrate on assisting the two girls on the long walk still to be made. There was no longer need of their being tied together and Lynch removed the rope, coiling it around his big waist. Behind the soldiers and her father Ann Ryan slogged doggedly, head down to follow the trench in the snow. Price moved against Sue Steelman, supporting her in one arm, half carrying her but keeping her feet on the ground, forcing her to use her legs and feet though she sagged heavily against him.

Lynch set a steady snail pace, giving the exhausted blonde what relief he could and still make progress. It was much longer than the two hours he had estimated before he called back along the column that Fort Sedgwick lay in sight.

Price lifted his eyes from watching the track. Ahead the stars appeared to hover just on the rolling horizon. But there was a dark band between one cluster of them and the vast display above. That then would be the fort, another mile southwest. He murmured the encouragement to Sue Steelman. She gave no sign that she heard, out on her feet, moving only because the Captain kept her going.

It was a last long mile. The lights grew clearer. The bulking shape of a stockade surrounding the post loomed up, a fence of stout logs set on end, their tops cut to sharp points like teeth against the silver sky. Through the wide, open gate Price made out the snow-covered, familiar pattern within, the parade, the stables, enlisted men's barracks, officers' quarters. Almost there, he saw the sentry box just outside the gates, saw three figures silhouetted against the background lights.

Safety was there. Heat. Warm drink and food. Sergeant Mike Lynch had delivered on his promise of escape. Captain Jack Price would immediately request a citation for the ingenuity, resourcefulness, perseverance of the man. But even the doughty Sergeant no longer had breath to call ahead. It was left to the sentries to discover the dark shapes moving across the snow toward them. When they did one shouted, sounding astonished.

"Halt. Who goes there?"

Lynch plodded closer, not answering until he could do so in a voice that could be heard. The sentries unslung their rifles, leveled them, spaced themselves across the gateway. The first speaker repeated his command in a harsher tone. Lynch stopped ten feet away, filled his lungs and grated.

"Me. Sergeant Lynch. With the last people from Julesburg. Indians there. Thousand anyway."

Without turning his head the sentry spoke to the side. "Haney, bring the lantern," and to the party arriving, "Advance and be recognized, with your hands over your heads."

In view of his late experiences in this country Captain Price considered the caution admirable, and the blue uniforms had never looked more welcome. With one arm tight around Sue Steelman he raised the other high, spreading the fingers to show they were empty, and walked another five feet closer. The sentry sent for a light brought the lantern from the guard box, holding it up to show the party's faces. It also showed the faces of the men facing them.

Lynch said in a stronger voice, "You're new on this post? I don't know any of you."

There was something near laughter in the other's tone. "We're new. Don't know you either. Haney, Burns, disarm them, then we'll march them in and make sure of them."

Lynch swore a protest but kept his hands up and submitted to having his guns taken, removed to the sentry box. The two troopers, Ryan, and Price were all stripped of weapons. While that was being done Price appealed to the sentry in charge.

"Soldier, these women have walked five miles through the blizzard. In the name of God take them to the mess and get something hot into them before they collapse."

Dark as it was outside the gate the man identified the two figures bundled in buffalo robe and sheepskin long coat as females belatedly.

Starting, he said, "Of course. Ladies, go with Private Burns here. Burns, come back straightaway."

The private hung his gun on his shoulder, walked to Price and held his hand toward Sue Steelman. Price took his arm from around her, holding her elbow, but she sank toward the ground. The private was quick, scooping her up, carrying her across his chest, saying, "Come along, miss," to Ann, taking them across the parade toward the long kitchen and officers' mess building.

Ann walked beside them, her back straight, her head up, still strong and poised although Price knew she must be at least as tired as he. There were other soldiers in a group on the parade who turned to watch the arrival with distinct interest and Burns turned the girls over to them for care, jogging back to the gate, where the rest of the party was still held under guns. Since Sergeant Lynch and his two troopers were all in uniform it seemed to Price an unnecessary delay in the cold, jittery as this post might be about the massive Indian uprisings since the Salt Creek massacre. By no stretch of imagination could any of them be mistaken as tribesmen. Yet if these sentries were new in the service they were probably following an order to the letter. Lynch was not so patient, swearing now that the women were out of earshot.

"What the hell is this, Private? Let's get indoors. I've got to report to Captain Sanders."

Again Price sensed laughter under the sentry's words as Burns trotted up. "We'll go see the Commander now, Sergeant. But until you're all identified just keep your hands up."

He jerked his head toward the gate, stood by while the party filed through, then, leaving a single sentry on guard, he and Burns followed as Lynch stormed toward the quarters of the commanding officer, leading the group.

Crossing the parade with both hands held at shoulder level, Price had a first premonition that all was not as it should be here. He had been too relieved to arrive at the post, too concerned for the girls to have noticed before, but now he heard the sentries' voices in echo, soft, slurred tones associated with Virginians. And what were Southerners doing in blue coats? Northern sympathizers choosing to support the Union rather than the rebellion? There were many such of course, but the Captain felt a prickle at his hairline.

At the porch of the two-story log building the sentry passed the group, took the steps first, knocked on the door and at a summons from inside opened it and stepped through and to one side. Price saw the salute snapped, heard the announcement.

"Party from Julesburg, sir. Sergeant Lynch with a report of massive Indian attack there. He says."

Price was next to last into the room, blocked in the doorway because Lynch and the two troopers had brought up short just inside the entrance. Behind him Burns prodded his back with the rifle.

"Go on. Go on. You want to freeze the Captain?"

Price put a hand on Ryan's shoulder, shoved him gently and they sidestepped the troopers enough that Burns could crowd in and close the door, his attention held on Lynch. The Sergeant was saluting but sounding strangled.

"Sir? Captain Sanders, where is he?"

"Chasing Indians, Sergeant. I am Captain Calhoun in temporary command. At your service."

There was no doubt about laughter in this captain's deep drawl. It was rich with amusement. Price swung his eyes quickly to the man at the desk facing Lynch, his profile to Jack Price. He knew well the name Calhoun. He knew the face. They had been classmates at West Point. But through the grapevine he had heard that Calhoun had joined the rebel army at the outbreak of the war.

Price opened his mouth to give a warning, then closed it,

clamped his lips tight. All of them were disarmed, tricked into surrendering their guns, and the two sentries' rifles were steady on the Sergeant. He stood very still, not to draw attention to himself, listening while Lynch, still unsuspecting, made his report of the detail's sortie, of its heavy losses, of the remnant's and the others' escape from the Julesburg station. But something, some awakening warning that came as he spoke caused him to neglect any mention of the girls or Jack Price's name. He finished on a dazed note and stood gaping at Calhoun.

The man at the desk acknowledged the report, complimented Lynch on his performance, then for the first time looked at the survivors. His glance passed briefly over the two troopers and Ryan, touched Price, went to the sentries, swept back to Price and held there in recognition. Calhoun took in the civilian clothes, his mouth thinning to a hard line before he rose in a slow, even movement, walked to the door and beckoned Burns outside with him.

They were gone only a moment, then Calhoun returned to the desk, saying, "Take them over where they can eat and sleep." He pointed at Price and added, "All except this man. I'll talk with him first."

CHAPTER FIVE

Sergeant Mike Lynch saluted at attention, about-faced and stepped toward the door, his eyes on Price dark and troubled. Price barely nodded and saw the Sergeant's big face flush with anger as he marched out of the office with the others and the sentries behind him.

The two captains, alone in the room, were silent, looking at each other for long moments. Virgil Calhoun was of an age with Jack Price, a handsome yellow-haired man who wore the blue uniform with the same rakish ease as he had at the Point, a courtly, elegantly mannered man. Jack Price had a blazing urge to jump the desk, grab for the sidearm in Calhoun's holster, tear off the coat. Even at the Point he had strongly disliked Calhoun, was admittedly jealous. The cadet had had everything, money, social position, charm that made women fawn over him. Price had never understood why such a person should choose the Army as a career. The family was of St. Louis, where they controlled many of the boats that plied the great river. The mother was heir to a large plantation in Mississippi and Virgil's boyhood had been spent in the slave state; his background was steeped in the slave psychology that was so unwholesome to Price. Most galling had been Sue Steelman's closeness to the Southerner. Though she flirted with all the cadets, Calhoun had clearly held the inside track. They might have married had not General Steelman, watching the deterioration between North and South, foreseen where Calhoun's sympathies must lie, and forbade his daughter that choice of husband.

What explained Captain Virgil Calhoun sitting at this desk dressed in blue, not gray? With other Southerners apparently controlling this fort? It flashed on Price that there could be only one answer. These were the guerrillas whom Ben Holladay had said were harassing the Overland. Price was their prisoner. A weakness attacked his knees. He stepped to the chair opposite Calhoun and sank down on it, hypnotized as by a cobra.

Outside a sudden commotion erupted, Lynch's bull roar, outraged, other yells, a shot. Price lunged to his feet, headed for the door, forgetting he had no gun. Calhoun's voice, laughing again, stopped him.

"Sit down, Jack. It's all right. Just your sergeant objecting to being quartered in the guardhouse. Probably fought against it and the shot was a warning." And as Price sagged back on the chair, his hands tight on the arms, Calhoun went on laconically. "What are you doing here, in those clothes?"

Price drew a long breath, taking himself in tight control to match the other's easy manner. "A long story and not worth the telling." He had no intention of saying why he was in Colorado and out of uniform. If Calhoun jumped to the conclusion that he was no longer in the Union Army, so much the better.

"Strange." Calhoun smiled. "Running into you here this

way. Burns said there are two women with you. Who are they?"

"Stranger than you know, Captain." Price's mouth turned up on one side. "One is Ryan's daughter from Julesburg station. The other is Sue Steelman."

That brought the Southerner jolting to his feet. "Sue? At Sedgwick? Why?"

"Her father wanted her with relatives in Denver while he took the field. If you were the 'Indians' who killed people at the swing stations you missed finding her at Big Spring. She was hiding there."

The color drained from Calhoun's face. He dropped heavily to his chair, his composure gone, his expression a clear admission of his guilt, passing a hand over the wet that started from his face.

He said hoarsely, "I didn't know . . ."

Price said in a flat voice, "You do now, damn you. And she is here. Unless there's a garrison upward of a thousand you'd better get us all out of here tonight before we're overrun. What did you do with the Union men here?"

Calhoun shook off his shock and his blue eyes turned bleak. "They're mostly out patrolling, only found a handful when we came in, a corporal, four troopers and the cook. We're at war, Price."

Seething, Jack Price bit out his words. "You killed them? Six defenseless men?"

"Hardly defenseless. They fought. I lost four good boys. Price, don't look at me that way. We buried them honorably, just before the blizzard hit. We'd have been gone by now except for it."

Price's face remained hard, cold. "And will you bury us before you leave?"

Calhoun sighed at the demands war made on a man. "I won't have to. Sue . . . she'd ask too many questions if we went off without your bunch. Get a night's sleep. We'll pull out sometime tomorrow."

"Virgil." Price leaned forward for emphasis. "At dawn tomorrow those tribes at Julesburg will find the station empty and start for here. What is it, five miles? Do you intend to wait around for them?"

The Southerner shrugged. "There's no hurry. You know how much liquor Ben Holladay stocks his stations with? Enough to keep that war party drunk for a week, and if you know anything about Indians, you know they'll travel farther for a bottle of firewater than they will for a scalp. They'll be days up there."

Footsteps clumped up to the porch. Calhoun raised his voice to order the man inside and the sentry Burns stepped smartly through the door. Without taking his eyes off Price, Calhoun told Burns to find Lieutenant Reeves and send him here. When the officer arrived and the sentry had retired, Calhoun introduced the Lieutenant and added,

"Meet Jack Price. Late of the Union Army, for what reason I have not yet learned. Keep an eye on him while I go on an errand, but do not talk with him." He reached for the bottom desk drawer, brought up a bottle and two glasses, set them forward. "One drink for you, Lloyd, but let him have all he wants."

Jack Price touched a finger to his hatbrim just before Calhoun went out, grateful for the hospitable gesture though he suspected the idea was to make him garrulous. He was traveling on his nerve, half frozen, sick with exhaustion and the discoveries found at this post. The whiskey would be more than welcome. He watched the Lieutenant pour two glasses, shove one at Price and sit down in the opposite chair with the other, sipping it, his distant attention on the prisoner.

The Captain raised his glass, swallowed the whole content at once, felt the raw liquor fiery in his throat and stomach as he offered the glass for a refill. His mind followed Virgil Calhoun across the parade toward a reunion with Sue Steelman. Seeing him dressed in blue, she would not know the duplicity and he was sure no one would alert her. Would she go to his arms as willingly as she had to Price at Big Spring? And was it tiredness that kept the stir of jealousy so faint, or had seeing her in a fresh light these last days cured him of the hold she had once had?

That was not his immediate concern. His foremost thought was whether, believing Calhoun to be what he appeared, Sue would tell him Price was still with the Army. She had said she would not tell anyone, she was the daughter of a Union general, and he pinned his hope on that that she would not betray him. If Calhoun thought he was a deserter or cashiered out, Price might not be watched too closely. He might find an unguarded moment to escape, to warn the Army headquarters in Denver. And the girls would be safe enough under the protection of this Southern gallant, whatever disposition Calhoun might determine for the Northern troopers and Vance Ryan.

The two drinks were taking hold, muddying his thinking. He could no longer follow a train of ideas. Abruptly his body loosened and he was asleep in the chair. He was not conscious of the Lieutenant summoning the sentry, of being hoisted between them and walked to the guardhouse, where the other male members of the escape party were already snoring on the hard bunks.

Reveille brought them all groaning, fighting to dull wakefulness. While one guard leveled a rifle on them outside the barred cell, another unbolted the grating, bringing a pail of cold water, setting it on the bench beside the tin basin, a third brought hot food and steaming coffee. The icy water on his face cleared Price's head somewhat. He ate the beans ravenously, silent with the others, who wolfed at the plates. When those and the mugs were empty the guard gathered the tinware, reached Price last and stopped before him.

"Captain wants you in his office."

Sergeant Lynch, with the guard's back toward him, cocked one eyebrow high in an unspoken question that Price had no way to answer except with a small shrug as he stood up. He covered that by feeling through his pockets for his pipe, which was gone, dropped probably in the spills and scrambles on the river ice.

Stiff, aching, he walked ahead of the guard into the shocking brilliance of the first sunrays reflected off the snow-covered parade. Blinded by the glare, he fumbled for direction until the guard prodded him toward the headquarters building and up the porch steps he could barely see, knocked, and at Calhoun's call opened the door, spread a hand in Price's back and shoved him through.

By contrast to the bright parade the room was dark. It was over a minute before Price could make out the Southerner seated behind the desk as he had been the night before, the handsome face more wary, mockery twisting his delicate lips.

Calhoun did not speak until they were alone, until he was sure the other's eyes had adjusted to the gloom, then his voice came hard, distant.

"Sit down, Captain. We are equal as officers."

Price lowered himself into the facing chair, his hope sinking that his status would remain concealed, automatically again patting his pockets for the pipe, then as he remembered dropping his hands to his knees.

"Looking for a smoke?" Calhoun sounded more jaunty, opened the humidor on the desk, gathered a handful of cigars and passed them across, then emptied the box into his jacket pockets. He struck a match and held it toward Price. "Your C.O. here had a taste for good tobacco, and he must have had funds other than his army pay. Enjoy one with me."

Price saw nothing to be gained by refusing and the taste, the aroma, filled a strong need at the moment, helping to settle the churning inside him. Since Sue Steelman had given him away, he must quickly reorder his answers to the questions that would soon come.

Calhoun was not long about it, waiting only until the tip of his cigar was cherry red and he blew out the first inhalation of blue smoke.

"You know the penalty of a soldier being caught behind enemy lines in wartime, *Captain*."

Price said evenly, "I am not behind enemy lines. You are. This is a Union post."

Virgil Calhoun's smile was wide and wicked, his eyes bird bright. "Not today. Not since yesterday morning. This fort is now held for the Confederate States of America. Now, tell me what is this detached duty that brings you to Colorado out of uniform."

Price damned Sue Steelman. She had not only told the Southerner his present rank but had enlarged with everything she knew. His only recourse was to keep silent. Calhoun let the moments run, dribbling smoke, his eyes fast on Price. Finally he rubbed a long ash onto the tray, crossed his arms on the desk, leaning forward.

"I can make a sharp guess, Jack. I am not a fool. You were sent to run down rumors that we were raiding as Indians to wreck Holladay's operation. We'd have accomplished it without your idiot Chivington at Sand Creek bringing out every redskin on the Plains. Now we'll have to interrupt the action for a while, return to Denver. We'll find out from you there whether the guess is on target or you're after something else. First, we have some chores here. May I have your word not to try an escape?"

Slowly Jack Price shook his head. "You know better, Virgil."

Calhoun shrugged, expecting the refusal. "Of course, though I had to ask. It would make it easier for all of us." He called the sentry and ordered Price returned to the guardhouse.

Back in that confine Price sat down close to Sergeant Lynch, in a low voice laying out the whole situation, including what his Washington orders had been and the reason for them, while Lynch rumbled his fury. Price moved on from one to another, repeating, cautioning them all to say nothing, but if any one of them could get away on the trip he must report to the Army in Denver. The sentry was suspicious, watching through the bars, alert, his gun held ready to stop any attempted break.

Through the morning the compound was busy. Men went from building to building making preparations. A Union caisson was loaded with ammunition, harnessed to a team and taken out through the gate. A wagon was filled with foodstuffs, also hitched and driven outside. A sleigh was made ready for travel, equipped with robes and tied before the building where Price assumed the two girls were quartered. Horses enough for all the men were saddled, kept within the stockade. All other mounts, a considerable number of replacements belonging to the fort, were driven out as a herd.

At noon the activity stopped and the deceptive garrison and prisoners were fed. Afterward Virgil Calhoun escorted Sue Steelman and Ann Ryan to the sleigh, tucked them into the seat behind the driver, who climbed up, took the reins and walked the rig sedately through the gate.

Lynch, the troopers and Ryan were taken from the cell one at a time, mounted, their wrists tied to the low pommels, their feet fastened by lines under the animals' bellies and two Southerners with drawn rifles escorted them after the sleigh, well behind it. Price was given a horse and not tied but left waiting with a single guard. He knew a temptation to bolt but it was unreal to expect he could get clear and his death would serve nothing at this point.

Captain Calhoun stepped to his saddle, put his horse near Price's and issued his orders through his lieutenant. Besides that officer Price counted two sergeants and thirty horses ready for the troopers in a column two by two. Half of these men were ordered up, the others sent on foot through the compound buildings and around the base of the stockade.

Price saw smoke begin to curl from doors and windows, flames lick up the resin-saturated logs that surrounded the post. As the men finished their tasks of firing Sedgwick, they came to the column and mounted. The last one arrived at a run and threw himself to his saddle. Calhoun lifted a hand, wheeled to the head of his troop and took it out through the gate at a fast pace with Jack Price at his side.

The wagons, the sleigh, the riders and extra horses were gathered in a loose scatter on a low hill a mile away to the south. Calhoun headed that way. They had covered only half the distance when a great explosion erupted behind them. Turning in the saddle, Price saw a volcano of flame, smoke and debris thrown high above the spiked stockade top and knew the ammunition magazine had blown. Billows of smoke from the buildings and wall told him that nothing would be left standing by nightfall. He heard Virgil Calhoun's soft, slurred words as the Southerner also watched the holocaust.

"That too will be credited to avenging Indians, Jack. Now we will return to Denver and other duty."

Price kept his voice toneless, crowded down his great anger at this devastation. "Is that why you brought all the horses along? Because Indians are always after army horses?"

The other Captain smiled, a thin, self-satisfied pull at his lips. "That's one reason. Another, for protection. As you say, the braves are always hungry for animals, and with so many of them on the warpath we may run into a party large enough to give us trouble. If we drop these off in small bunches I'd guess they'd stop chasing us to pick them up, gain us time to leave them behind."

They rode on to the waiting cluster of people and vehicles. Calhoun ordered Price to position himself beside the sleigh and turned off to form a traveling unit of his band. These guerrillas would have taken their training along the bloody Kansas-Missouri border. They were murderers all, killers of civilians there and along the Overland's route. Yet they followed their leader with as precise discipline as Price had ever seen in any company of soldiers. Grudgingly he had to admit that whatever else Virgil Calhoun was he was a thoroughly competent commander as he set his troop in motion without confusion, without delay, each man and wagon slipping into place with a fluid grace, the extra horses hazed in a bunch at the back of the column.

CHAPTER SIX

Jack Price moved forward, past his fellow prisoners, their mounts fastened together in single file by a lead line tied at the rear of the sleigh so the Southerners need not lessen their slim strength by detailing guards specifically for them. The column was split, half riding on one side of the vehicles, half on the other so that they were effectively flanked. The Northern Captain came abreast of the sleigh, choosing the side on which Ann Ryan rode, and smiled warmly at her, not knowing whether she was aware of their actual situation, wanting to warn her. The flash of her dark eyes showed him no warning was needed.

Sue Steelman leaned across the other girl toward Price, delight and childish excitement shining in her face, saying lightly, "Jack, it's like a miracle, first you appearing out of the air, then Virgil. I feel really safe now with this many soldiers. Did you two burn the fort to keep Indians from getting it, all the guns and equipment I mean?"

Ann Ryan's lips twisted, her brows went up in irony. "I couldn't stop her, Captain." The tone was low with apology. "She blurted the whole thing out as soon as she saw him. Stood with his arms around her and delivered you to him as a head on a plate. I hope she did not understand what she was doing."

"I'm sure she did not, Ann." Price was solemn. "Is this the first she has heard about it from you?"

"Yes. I didn't want her to know I knew. Just in case she's on his side."

"And how did you know?"

Her full lips turned scornful. "Obvious, wasn't it? The way they talk, their mouths full of mush?"

Sue Steelman, looking from one to the other in growing bewilderment, cut in. "What's obvious? Whatever are you talking about?"

Ann Ryan settled back, leaving it to Price to say what must be said to the General's daughter, and Price said quietly, as gently as he could,

"Sue, Virgil Calhoun is a captain, but in the Southern army . . ."

"He is not. His uniform . . ."

"They captured Fort Sedgwick, took the uniforms from there. We're all prisoners, and now that he knows I am on duty my chances are slimmer of doing anything to help."

Her eyes stared, blazing, her flush was not at all pretty, she made several false starts before she could snap at him.

"I don't believe you, Jack Price. Virgil is a gentleman who would never behave that way."

Still he was patient. "See for yourself, Sue. Look behind at Ryan and the troopers who brought you out of Julesburg. They're tied in the saddles, roped together, tied to this sleigh."

The blond girl flung the robe off her lap, flung around to kneel on the seat, bent over the high curved back. In the frozen moments while the truth penetrated to her brain

Ann Ryan and Jack Price looked deeply into each other's face exchanging messages, the dark-haired girl still suspicious that Sue Steelman was a Southern spy in spite of Price's small negative move of his head.

"She's not that aware," he said in a low tone, but saw one eyebrow lift again.

Before Ann could argue Sue swung back, covered her lap and stared straight ahead, speechless, isolated in an invisible cocoon, not even glancing at the other girl or Price, and they continued in silence.

Captain Calhoun skirted the stream, never more than a couple of hundred yards from the icebound course, paralleling the low hills, with flankers far out in front to bring warning if they found Indians or Union patrols. It was some forty miles to Sterling, the first town of any consequence, and they were making good time. The glittering snow was not deep enough to slow the horses: in fact it was a help, packing over the ice sheet left by previous winter storms. Except ahead of the column where he could not see Price could find no sign of tracks, human, equine or even animal, anywhere on the white wasteland.

At noon Calhoun called a half-hour rest, a fireless camp that would not raise smoke to draw an attack. Cold biscuit and jerky with canteen water were distributed. Virgil Calhoun took portions to the girls, who stayed in the sleigh, and lingered at Sue Steelman's side. Dismounted and watching from a distance that he could cover quickly but was out of earshot, Jack Price waited for the blonde to confront the Southerner. She was faced away from him so he could not tell how she looked, but Calhoun, handing over the food, removed his wide hat, smiled and continued smiling. Price saw him shrug, saw his lips move, saw him reach for and hold her hand, speaking earnestly, and finally saw Sue settle back, an arch tilt to her head, relaxation in her whole figure. Ann Ryan kept her face averted and down, chewing deliberately at the tough fare.

It was too much when Price heard Sue Steelman laugh. He pivoted and marched toward the belt of cottonwoods along the stream. Screened there, he relieved himself, noting that the Lieutenant and a sergeant had followed with drawn guns.

He said in contempt, "Afraid I'll run for it?"

The Sergeant looked sheepish, uncertain. The Lieutenant did not. He was young with only the beginning of a dragoon mustache he was trying to cultivate.

He said harshly, "No telling what a damn fool Yankee might try. Get back to camp."

It was Price's first real awareness of the officer, barely out of boyhood, and what he saw was chilling. There was a wild restlessness about the eyes, the paleness of icebergs, and the tragic war that had taught him violence had found an eager scholar. Price read in the tic at the corner of his mouth that the blood he had tasted had whetted an appetite that would never be wholly satisfied however long his life lasted. Some latent strain within him had been fanned to fire. A killer had been created. Jack Price moved obediently back to the others, almost expecting a bullet between his shoulders to be explained as stopping an escape.

As they got under way again Captain Virgil Calhoun

motioned Captain Jack Price to the head of the column to ride at his side. He made no explanation but it was not hard to guess that the Southerner did not want the Northerner talking against him to Sue Steelman. Price wondered what Calhoun had told her to put her at such ease that she would laugh with him as though he were still a close friend and not the enemy.

From the new position he had a forward view of unbroken snow, a rolling white sheet marred only by the tumbled lines of the flankers' tracks far out on either side. With the miles lengthening between them and Julesburg his morning's uneasiness relaxed. He gave up glancing back in suspicion of finding the big Indian war party bearing down on them, and he sensed a lift from tension in the column.

There had been no sign of savages when at dusk they entered an irregular street between a huddle of log cabins and board and batten stores. As at Julesburg there were no lamps lighted, no one in evidence. Sterling had apparently not been raided yet but its people had fled.

Calhoun deployed his troop in the cabins nearest the stage swing station, took the girls, his cook and Price into the little building, ordered what horses the small corral would hold closed inside that and the rest held in a rope enclosure under strong guard for the night. The other prisoners Price supposed were billeted in a cabin. He heard Calhoun's command that no fires be built, no lights made. Only the cook was permitted to heat the station stove, make a hot meal after dark, when smoke would not show outside and the windows were draped with blankets.

The four within the station were served first, fried meat and sour dough biscuits, army beans and weak but hot coffee. It was a silent, uncomfortable supper with even Calhoun restraining whatever he might have said without Price listening, but his eyes played warmly on Sue Steelman across the table. Ann Ryan was withdrawn, her attention on the plate before her, obviously critical of the General's daughter and the Southern Captain.

When they had finished the guerrillas came in, four at a time, eating in relays, the last contingent carrying food away to Ryan and the Union troopers. Calhoun had ushered the two girls into the single bedroom, where they need not be ogled by his men, and when even the cook was gone he told Price shortly,

"Your choice of where you sleep, Jack. On the floor here or a bunk with your friends."

Price found a cool smile. He did not want to leave Calhoun in a position where he might spend the evening further courting the blond girl, and wondered that the Southerner gave him this option. It was Ann Ryan's presence, he judged, that was a restraining factor on the man. He did not answer, only shook out the blanket roll he had brought from the horse he had ridden, took it to the kitchen and wrapped himself in it close to the stove. Calhoun went out for a final round of inspection, then joined Price on the far side of the warm range.

Price pretended sleep for a long while, debating. If Calhoun slept heavily perhaps he could slip out through the rear door, take the sentry there by surprise and make an escape. But in the end he gave the idea up. There were low voices beyond the door. More than one man on guard there and it was unlikely he could avoid two or more.

He could not say when he drifted off or how long he had slept when a commotion roused him outside, shouts, and soon a guerrilla came in from the front, his boots loud on the floor planks, calling softly.

"Captain, Lieutenant Reeves requests you join him at the prisoners' cabin."

In the dark kitchen Price heard Calhoun rise immediately and rolled to his feet himself to follow, but the Southerner stopped him.

"You stay here. Sentry, watch that he doesn't try to leave."

Worry and guessing would do no good, whatever was happening. Price struck a match, took a mug from the shelf against the wall, poured lukewarm coffee from the pot on the cooling stove and sat down with it at the table. One-handed the sentry poured himself a cup and stood with it across the room, his short gun leveled, the barrel winking, caught by the last bright coals showing through the draft grating of the firebox.

Calhoun was not long. He came back, lighted the lamp and turned it very low, got coffee for himself, discovered a whiskey bottle on the shelf where the mugs sat and laced all three drinks, telling the sentry,

"Put it down pronto, then you're relieved here."

While the man tossed the drink back, saluted and left, Calhoun took the chair across from Price with a dry chuckle.

"Your sergeant is a card, Jack. Thought he could play

the same game with us he did with the Indians. Got outside and jumped one guard before the other knocked him cold and raised an alarm for help to handle the other three. Even if he'd got loose where would he think he could go? How long would he last in this country without a gun? I'm glad you have better sense. Don't change your mind now because I doubled the guard to four men on every door."

Jack Price said nothing, reached for the bottle and added another heavy slug to the cup, drank it in a long swallow as a toast to Sergeant Mike Lynch, who did not give up until he was overwhelmed, and hoped that the ice-eyed Lieutenant had not mauled him badly. For himself he would not try to make his break until there were better odds of success than he had yet seen. Warmed by the liquor, he rolled in the blanket again to finish the night.

It was the black dark that precedes dawn's gray when the cook arrived, waked the officers as he built up the fire, turned the lamp higher. Again Calhoun called in a sentry to watch Price, went to rouse the girls, left the building to get the sleeping men up without risking the sound of a bugle that could carry to Indians in the neighborhood.

Price rolled his blanket, took it and a chair to a corner out of the cook's way, welcoming the warmth as the stove took the bitter chill from the small kitchen. He breakfasted there without seeing either girl or the Southerners as they took their turns in the dining room. It was a relief when he saw four servings sent out to the cabin, indicating that Lynch was in good enough shape to eat.

The cook did not stay to clean the kitchen and it was up to each man to wash his tin plate, steel fork, and tin mug in the stream and stow them in his saddlebag. Price washed his and the sentry's in the pail beside the kitchen sink, gave the man his utensils, gathered up his blanket roll and went outside.

In the station yard the girls were already tucked in the sleigh, the rig ready to move. Men were finishing their saddling and mounting. Price cinched on his saddle, fastened the blanket roll behind it and stepped up. The shadows were still deep but he could make out figures on horseback clustered around the cabin doorway. He had turned his horse that way when Lynch's outraged roar shattered the early quiet.

"What the hell do you mean, leave us here, you scurvy renegade? Put us afoot in this no-place?"

Calhoun's hard voice mocked him as Price came up. "You wanted to get free, didn't you? I am freeing you. All four of you. You're no good to me and you only tie up my men watching you. If we run into Indians I'll need every one fighting. Perhaps you'd rather I executed you?"

Jack Price told the Captain in full scorn, "You didn't learn that kind of honor at the Point, Calhoun. Leaving anyone in this place is a death sentence by itself."

There was a flurry of movement and in the gloom Ann Ryan pushed through the mounted men to the prisoners, turned to face Calhoun as tall as she could stretch herself.

"Your true colors show now, Captain. And if you abandon my father and these soldiers I stay with them. Rather the Indians than the company of such brutes."

Sue Steelman came running just behind Ann, hugging the furry robe about her, stopping at Calhoun's stirrup, saying in a shocked tone, "Virgil Calhoun, you wouldn't? And you call yourself a gentleman? If you do that I'll never speak to you again."

"Sue"—the Southerner showed a sudden impatience— "we are in a war and these are my enemy. Also, I have the responsibility of getting you safely to Denver. I cannot be hampered by prisoners who will not give their word not to try escape again. There's too much danger in taking them any further."

Price recognized the man's dilemma, the military fact that Calhoun had no other realistic choice, for if this little band were attacked by a large Indian force he could not afford the burden of men he could not trust.

Sergeant Lynch swore at the Southerner. "At least leave us guns, some self-defense."

"So you can shoot us in the back when we ride out? I think not, Sergeant. Be still now."

A solution of sorts came to Price, less than he wished for but the best he could find and he said flatly, "Captain, you can leave guns and ammunition at the south edge of town. Tie the men loosely here so you can be out of range by the time they have the ropes off and reach the weapons." Looking at Ann Ryan, he went on. "They can keep out of sight here today and walk by night, take food with them so they won't need to fire at game. Calhoun, where is the danger to you in that?"

The Southerner watched him in the growing light, studying the idea, searching for some treachery in it, then his lips turned up a trifle.

"You always could find a cute answer, Price. All right. Burns, some of you lash these men to the corral fence.

Lieutenant Reeves, see that the ladies are escorted into the sleigh and kept there. When we drop off guns for the Yankees you stay there half an hour on guard, then rejoin us."

"No." Jack Price's voice was harsh. "Not Reeves. Someone else. Your lieutenant would enjoy murdering these people with no one to stop him."

He read in Calhoun's face that this had been the Southerner's explicit intention, that with the girls off the scene there would be no constraint on the young killer. But in their presence Price's accusation spoiled that game. Calhoun glared at him for a long moment, then surrendered with an attempt at grace for the benefit of Sue Steelman, ordered Reeves only to stand over the guns until the column was safely away.

The blond girl looked from one captain to the other, appalled at this glimpse of what war was, then walked unresisting to the sleigh. Ann Ryan fought the two guerrillas who took her arms and finally lifted her clear of the ground, carrying her across the yard, forcing her up to the seat and holding her there while the driver shook the horse to a run. Price saw Sue Steelman turn to look back and raise her hand in a tentative wave, but did not know for whom it was intended.

Only when they were well gone did Calhoun order Price's hands roped to the pommel, his feet tied in a malicious show of vengeance that he explained as a precaution against this prisoner giving him trouble. Then he took his column out of the yard to run the long Indian-scourged corridor to Denver.

CHAPTER SEVEN

A mile south of town the column halted, waiting until Lieutenant Reeves had made a dashing run to catch up, pass it, salute his captain, and make his report. Price saw him back his horse off to the side and hold there as Calhoun raised an arm, swept it forward and moved out again.

Reeves sat rigid until Price came abreast of him, riding near the rear of the guerrillas, flanked on both sides, then the Lieutenant pushed through the line, took Price's rein from the man leading him and dropped on back of the riders the length of a horse. Price kept his face forward, his head up until Reeves laughed, a sound like glass breaking.

"Look at me, bucko."

Price turned his head, his expression empty. The pale eyes laid on him had a wicked eagerness, the thin lips a one-sided smile.

"Give me just the slightest excuse, Yankee, and I'll have a new scalp. That interference back there put you at the head of my list."

Price looked away, not answering the taunt. He had not needed to be put on notice. If an apparent accident could be arranged that would not throw the onus of his death on Virgil Calhoun it would be used. Only Sue Steelman's presence had deterred it so far. As a West Point graduate, Calhoun should be expected to follow the book regarding the treatment of prisoners of war, of officers on the opposing side, but the Southerner had thrown the book away in turning to outlaw tactics, in the murder of civilians, so why had Price not already been shot? He thought he could read jealousy in Calhoun of his friendship with the blond girl and a twisted pride that could not let her see or guess a treachery against the Northern Captain. Therefore, Price knew, he must obey to the letter any order given him, do nothing that even hinted at a plausible reason to execute him.

The march was paced to the wagons and teams, slowed by the slippery footing of snow churned to mushiness by the horses ahead. It made for tension all through the rank, a sense of vulnerability to attack. But the white plain was flat in all directions, affording no cover for hostiles until near noon when low, rolling mounds and gullies closed nearer on the east.

While those were still distant Calhoun made a stop to eat and to rest the animals. They built no fire because smoke might be seen by anyone behind the mounds, and they grouped the horse herd between the higher ground and the party. Lieutenant Reeves dismounted, untied Price's bonds and stood back to watch him step down. Hands numb from being unable to move them other than to flex the fingers, neither could take a firm grip on the horn, and when Price lifted his leg over the saddle, he fell ignominiously, dropping to the frozen ground as his foot gave way. The men around him laughed derisively. Mov-

ing with deliberate care, Jack Price got up, worked circula-
tion into his toes, walked to a spot Reeves indicated, away
from the mounts, and stood there quietly.

Cold fare was broken out, jerked meat and hard biscuit,
and water from canteens. Someone brought Reeves a serving, setting the tin plate on the snow where the Lieutenant
crouched with one hand resting on the butt of his belt gun.
The rest gathered at the wagon, where the cook was passing out rations. Virgil Calhoun carried plates to the sleigh;
he handed one to each of the girls and stood beside Sue
Steelman to eat and drink. Ann Ryan stood up, her eyes
seeking out Price; seeing his hands empty and no one
bringing him food, she got down and took her plate to him.

"Trash!" The word was explosive. "I saw you were tied.
Why did they think that necessary?"

Reeves was watching just out of earshot so Price did not
smile, but kept his voice soft, even. "Because I wouldn't
give my word not to try an escape. It's all right. Thanks for
the food. You'd better go get yourself some."

"Later. Thank you for seeing that Father and the boys
had guns. It gives them at least some chance, more than
you appear to have."

He did not want to talk about himself, not knowing
whether Reeves could read lips, and stayed with the subject of the station keeper and troopers.

"You know this country; what do you think your father
will do?"

She thought about that, frowning, but her head held
high. "Stay in Sterling today, and follow our tracks tonight. With the swath we're leaving their footprints won't

show. Tomorrow if they can make it beyond the snow where they won't leave a trail they'll turn west toward the mountains and the gold camps. From what we've heard the Indian action is mostly over east and after the blizzard even the foothills will be drifted too deep for their ponies." She looked back along the way they had come, at the wide path cut through the smooth white expanse by hoofs and wheels, and her tone turned bitter. "These Johnny Rebs, they're stupid. If that tribe at Julesburg goes on to the fort, they won't have to look for us. Drunk or not they can't possibly miss a trail like this. They travel light and fast, not hauling all this weight the *Captain* thinks he needs."

Price could not help smiling then, at her logic and her scorn. She had a mind and used it and he had not yet seen panic in her. As briefly as he had known her he felt a deep bond of warmth toward her. She did not have Sue Steelman's pampered prettiness but in her face and carriage there was solid strength that made her handsome to him.

"If you pointed out that reasoning to him the gallant gentleman might harken to a lady."

He saw decision tighten her firm lips and she turned away, walking smartly to the wagon where Virgil Calhoun was returning his soiled plate. She stood tall and straight before him and apparently read him a lecture. Wanting to hear, Jack Price ignored the watchdog Lieutenant and also went to the wagon. Calhoun was studying the back trail as Price came up, slowly nodding.

Price heard, "You could be right, Miss Ryan, but I am in command. We will keep the wagons until I see a need to leave them. In country as open as this we can't be

ambushed and any pursuit would be visible so far away
there would be time to take other action as required."

"Yes, you are in command, I am sorry to admit." The
girl was tart. "But you don't make sense. You are so casual
about Indians because you can see great distances. At the
same time, in the same geography, with all these men, you
truss up Captain Price in fright that he may run away.
Where could he run without being seen? Or are you purely
vindictive that he saved my father's life?"

Virgil Calhoun reddened, visibly annoyed by the criti-
cism, and threw a cold glance over the girl's shoulder at
Price, then turned on his heel and stalked away, pausing
for a word with Lieutenant Reeves.

Jack Price laughed softly as Ann Ryan came around to
face him, her large eyes still dark with anger.

"I don't believe Virgil is accustomed to being dressed
down by ladies of his acquaintance. It made my day even
if he puts a rope around my neck next."

She started. "Oh. I talk too much. I hope I haven't made
things even worse for you."

She had not. Reeves swaggered to him, jerking his head.

"Captain says throw your saddle on a fresh horse and
ride up front by him."

Price dropped one eyelid toward the girl without letting
Reeves see, then with the Lieutenant behind him he led
his horse to the remuda where the other men were
switching saddles and changing animals. Ann Ryan returned to the sleigh and got in, her face composed again,
not speaking to Sue Steelman.

The column moved out at the same pace as they had

kept through the morning, the sleigh at its head with Virgil Calhoun mounted afresh, riding at the blond girl's side, Price abreast of Ann Ryan with his wrists and ankles free. They exchanged glances, both amused, but neither risked a change of Calhoun's heart by talking. The girl had made an impression on the Southerner, not only shaming him into permitting Price the greater comfort of free movement but, Price noticed, causing him periodically to stand in his stirrups and look over the northern horizon.

No Indians had appeared by late afternoon when they rode out of the snow onto hard ground, frozen so that they no longer left tracks. At dusk they turned out of the road a mile to a bend in the Platte and a screen of cottonwoods to bivouac along the bank. Calhoun ordered a small fire built beside the river ice, hidden from the higher ground level. The cook made a hot meal while the detail chopped a trough through the ice, filled canteens and watered the animals.

It was full dark by the time they had eaten and beds had been made in a secluded area for the girls from the fur robes from the sleigh and extra blankets. Virgil Calhoun took pains to see that both were comfortable, still rankled by the Ryan girl's blow to his pride. When he was satisfied, keeping Jack Price with him, he posted sentries at points of vantage, including two with the horses corralled within a rope strung around trees, and delegated men to relieve them through the night. Back at the fire he squatted on his heels, motioning Price down opposite him.

"Get in the light where I can see your face, Jack. I want something understood between us. I can tie you to a tree

or you can listen to reason. If you think you can make a
break, get away in the dark through the woods, consider
this. Without a gun you can't get food. You can't defend
yourself if you run into redskins, which you probably
would. It's a very long hike down the river to Fort Morgan
and there's nothing in between here and there. You
couldn't make it. Which will it be, your word you won't
run, or the ropes?"

Price had talked over the possibility with Ann Ryan
while they ate. The road, she had said, followed the Platte
to Fort Morgan and below, then veered away south across
flat, empty plains to Denver. What might be found at Fort
Morgan could not be foretold: it could be burned out, and
if it was, if he reached it, he would have no chance of
crossing the plains alone and unarmed. It would be suicide
to try, a futile sacrifice. With that foreknowledge he did
not doubt Calhoun's warning and gave the Captain a small
smile.

"I believe you. Only because I've heard the same story
earlier. You have my word for tonight. Tell your Lieutenant not to back-shoot me if I get up in the dark."

Calhoun rose. "Come along and hear."

He offered a tentative hand as Price stood, but the
Northerner did not meet it.

"My word, I said. Nothing more."

Calhoun shrugged and walked to where Reeves sat
against a tree with his rifle across his lap, saying in a frosty
tone, "You are relieved of the watch, Lieutenant. Captain
Price has promised to stay with us until tomorrow without
restraints."

Price could not see Reeves's expression but his voice was incredulous.

"You believe him, Captain?"

"Certainly. He understands the choices and the odds against survival if he broke. I want him alive in the morning."

Reeves grunted, not liking the orders, a disappointed sound that relieved Price's suspicion of the killer's intent. The man would obey his captain.

The detail was settling down, tired after the day's tense riding. Jack Price chose an open spot at the edge of the cottonwood belt, rolled in his blanket and lay looking up. It was as if the big storm had washed the air to sparkling clarity. He had never seen a sky as brilliant as this arch above the high country, the star cloud swollen points of light as though he saw them through a magnifying glass. He should sleep, rest for the next day, but his mind would not relax, probing through the problems ahead.

How to get clear of Virgil Calhoun and his Southerners in blue. How to stop their depredations. They were headed for Denver and he wondered why, wondered how many Union troops were there and how Calhoun meant to deal with them. It being the capital of the state, the city must be well protected, so what made Calhoun believe he could avoid detection. Would they take Price into town? He thought not. There would be the risk that he might find a way to warn the Northerners that the detail was Confederate. And warn them he must or betray his nation. What of the girls, would they be less closely guarded than he, could they get a message across? Ann Ryan he trusted but

Sue Steelman was more likely to have some freedom because of Calhoun's interest in her. Yet he was not sure he could rely on her. Virgil Calhoun was handsome, courtly to women, and Sue lived on flattery. She had responded to his attentions all day, seeing him, Price suspected, as a romantic figure risking his life in the rebel cause. She herself might lean toward the Southern side or be politically neutral and she did not yet know it had been these men, not Indians, who had murdered and scalped at Big Spring station. If he told her would she believe him? If he could make her do that surely in revulsion she would make an effort to help.

He was not aware when the thoughts stopped and sleep came. It seemed an immediate transition from full wakefulness to being roused by a toe digging into his side, Reeves's acid order to roll out. He rose, groggy, chilled by the morning air, rolled his blanket and went to the river to splash ice water over his head and neck until his head cleared, then he went looking for Sue Steelman.

She had not yet come out of the retreat, and when she did appear, tousled, hugging the fur robe around her, Virgil Calhoun beat Price to her, bowed, laid his pocket comb across his forearm, offering it in the manner of surrendering his sword to a victor. She received it with a curtsy, sat on a fallen log combing her hair to a blond cascade that fell below her waist. Calhoun sat beside her and beckoned a man to bring breakfast for them. When the cups and plates were brought she ate daintily, laughing, as gay as if this were a picnic. Price would not be able to talk to her alone until a noon stop, if then. The Southern Captain had pre-empted her, whether for his entertainment, a renewal of their old courtship, or to separate her from any influence the Northerner could have on her was moot, and Price would have to find another approach.

He took a breakfast to Ann Ryan, increasingly impressed that she could look so fresh and calm while fully aware of their galling, dangerous situation.

"You've thought of something we can do." She looked through his eyes and read his mind.

"Possibly. If we are taken into Denver the Union troops there must be warned that these are rebel guerrillas. One of the three of us has to make a contact, and Calhoun is not likely to allow me the opportunity."

"Nor me." Ann mocked herself. "He knows too well what my opinions are. That leaves your Miss Steelman and the way she's behaving looks as though she's gone over to the other side."

"There could be another explanation, one I hadn't credited her with until last night. She is a Northern general's daughter, brought up in the tradition of loyalty. She could be playing a sly game of hypnotizing the enemy to quash his suspicion, win his confidence and a freer hand."

"Could be." The girl was thoughtful. "What few Southern belles I've seen are a wily lot who play with men for the sport. It's plain she's had plenty of exercise at it to make her expert. But how do we find out?"

"I think I know. I haven't told either of you this because it's ugly and you've both been through enough of that. Now, though, we can use it." He reached for her hand, held it tightly in her lap. "That butchery at Big Spring where we found Sue the only one left alive. Those were not Indian raiders, Ann. They were these so-called soldiers, under Captain Virgil Calhoun, made up as warriors."

It was well he had pressure on her fingers, increasing it as he finished. Through them he felt the involuntary start begin before her will controlled it. There was no visible sign of shock except a lengthening, deepening of her breathing. There was a time of silence while she steadied her speech, then it came in a whisper.

"You are certain? How?"

"The night at Fort Sedgwick Calhoun talked to me, asked who the women with us were. When I said Sue Steelman, that he had missed finding her when he attacked the station, he was too shaken to lie. He did not deny he was there. All he said was, *I didn't know.* I hadn't been sure. It was a shot in the dark."

Her eyes stayed on their hands where they would not betray her horror to anyone watching. It was long before she whispered again.

"She doesn't know?"

"No. If you could tell her, judge her reaction, we should learn where she stands."

He had to leave her then. The men were saddling, Reeves summoning him with the curt head jerk. They were on the way at sunup, Ann Ryan a quiet figure in the sleigh keeping her face toward Price, averted from the blond girl and the Southern Captain.

They crossed the river spread in a skirmish line to distribute the weight of the vehicles. Even so the caisson broke through the ice hub deep in the shallow water and a path had to be chopped clear to haul it out. They skirted Fort Morgan on the north through low hills, Calhoun not knowing whether or not there were troops there and not risking being seen. He pushed on without a noon break to be beyond the zone as quickly as possible, pausing only to change horses and pass around jerky and biscuit to be eaten in the saddle. It was twilight when they finally camped. Throughout the day there had been no moment when Ann could talk privately with Sue, and there was not until they retired.

In the morning over breakfast Price waited for Ann's report. It came in sharp disappointment.

"I told her all you said. She laughed at me. You are jealous of Calhoun, she insisted, trying to turn her against the Captain with a lie. It was so impossible that he would do such a thing that she would not even give the charge the credence of asking him for the truth. She told me to stay out of her affairs, said she had plans I should not interfere in. That was the only implication that she may be helping. So I still don't know which side she's on."

"And no way to learn except possibly by watching her." Price knew that even if he asked the blonde straight out he could not rely on an answer. It would be Sue jealous of his attentions to Ann, punishing him by keeping her intentions secret.

The day brought another forced march across the plain because of distant smoke signals seen once in the morning and once in the afternoon, but they were not attacked. Jack Price took some comfort that Sue was more reserved with Calhoun, catching her in calculating study of him when he did not know it, so possibly she did believe the Big Spring story but was keeping options of action open by not challenging him. He let her strictly alone.

Just before dark they found a sheltered rock bowl to hide in. With sentries on the rim in case the red men broke their habit of not fighting at night, they risked another fire.

Tired from two days of long, hard riding the detail bedded down immediately after eating. Virgil Calhoun saw the girls settled, then brought a bottle of brandy and cups to the fire where Jack Price sat looking into the embers puzzling over the General's daughter, thinking of what could lie ahead. Calhoun's mind too was on the future. He sat down, poured liquor for both and passed a cup across to Price, his smile broad.

"To Denver, Jack." He toasted his cup. "No Indians have hit us yet in spite of your spitfire's dire warning. And only one more day of travel if the luck holds."

"To Denver," Price repeated, drank and asked in curiosity, "Surely you don't expect to take the city with your handful of raiders?"

"We won't have to. Price"—Calhoun leaned forward, eager, nursing his cup in both palms, the smile spreading to a full grin, and spoke with soft emphasis—"there are *three thousand* Texans marching up from New Mexico. My orders are to contact them and guide them in. With that force we can hold Denver, block the Overland and cut Mr. Lincoln's country in two. If you behave you'll be free by summer."

There seemed no comment worth making. Jack Price kept his face empty, his eyes level on Calhoun. The Southerner sobered slowly, poured a second drink and sipped it without a toast, watching Price over the rim.

"We'll be riding into a crowded capital. I want your word that you won't try to holler an alarm. If you did that we'd have to shoot you and I don't want to. We were classmates too long. Without your promise you'll go in bound and gagged."

Jack Price sounded scornful, saying, "What makes you sure I'd keep such a promise? Soldiers do die that a nation may survive."

"Because I know you, know your type, the kind the Point was founded to foster. Your religion is honor, your word. You believe in it totally."

Price's brows went high on his forehead. Virgil Calhoun was of a breed that cherished honor fiercely, would kill a brother to defend it.

"You sound as if you don't."

Calhoun's head wagged slowly. "Not any longer. What I believe in now is my homeland. The right of my people to govern themselves as they see fit, not to lie under the boot heel of storekeepers. Our freedom is what I am fighting for."

Jack Price searched the handsome face, found no mark of savagery there and said in wonder, "You call what you are doing fighting?"

Captain Calhoun's chin went up defiantly. "Necessary tactics and effective, and whether you believe me or not we have hurt no women or children. For that you can accuse the Indians. What don't you approve of in our effort to shorten this inhumane war?"

"Your own inhumanity. Murder of civilians. Throwing the blame on the tribes who are fighting for their way of life too. There is no way to justify that, Virgil."

For a second there was agony in the Southerner's eyes, then they went flat, empty. He stood up, leaving the bottle, whether intentionally or forgetful because Price's thrust had struck too deep for peace of mind.

"You choose it hard. So be it."

In a military brace Calhoun walked away.

CHAPTER EIGHT

The last day out of Denver they passed one burned ranch in the morning and two clusters of buildings in the afternoon that from the distance looked intact. The troop was tense until at dark they raised the lights of the capital. The Southerners stopped then to tie Jack Price on his horse and bind a gag in his mouth, to put a lead line on the animal snubbed around Calhoun's horn, and to move half the detail forward ahead of the sleigh. Calhoun walked back to it. Price heard a commotion there and looked back. Calhoun's hands were on Sue Steelman's shoulders shaking her lightly in some argument. Ann Ryan sat stiffly as she was bound and gagged, moved to the floor and her robe spread to cover her. Then Calhoun had his way, tying Sue, easing her down, shaking her robe over her. The column proceeded then, Calhoun and Price at its head.

Short of the outskirts of town they were halted by a small group of home guard with fresh lighted torches. In the blue uniforms they were welcomed by shouts. Plainly the arrival of fresh soldiers eased the fear of a siege.

Allan Smith, leader of the patrol, saluted awkwardly, then discovered the bound man in civilian dress and said sharply, "Captain, sir, who's this?"

Calhoun's voice was flat. "Turncoat we caught with an Indian band. What's the situation here?"

The man waved the question aside. "How come you didn't hang him right off?"

Calhoun showed displeasure at the impertinence. "He hasn't given us the information he has."

Smith reached for the lead line. "Let us have him, sir, we'll wring him dry."

Calhoun was stiff. "No, thank you. It is military information. What is your report?"

Smith backed off, a small man whose importance shriveled under the army rebuff. He said that the Vigilance Committee of Ten, generally known as the Stranglers after their method of handling early day toughs, was managing what defense of the city was possible. He prayed to God there was no attack because only the civilian population was available to fight. No regular troops were left in the territory.

Virgil Calhoun bestowed a sardonic smile on Jack Price. Price had looked hard at each of the home guard represented here but none of them was in the least curious about him after Calhoun's lie. They accepted it at face value and were not alert to any signal he could pass, their minds absorbed by Indians. He turned his head to see the sleigh but it was surrounded by guerrillas, unnoticed by the men around the head of the column.

Calhoun kneed his horse, forcing the home guard to part, and took his party through them into the town. Riding down Larimer Street, Jack Price was startled at the brick buildings flanking both sides. Denver was a frontier town and he had imagined it a little larger replica of Julesburg. Belatedly he remembered that besides being a capital this was the central supply point for all the mining camps scattered through the mountains, and the volume and value of goods passing through the local merchants' hands was enormous. What dismayed him was to find no one on the dark streets with whom he might in some way communicate.

Watching him search the sidewalks, Calhoun chuckled, understanding the purpose. "No help for you here, is there? Governor's curfew keeps everybody indoors at night until the scare is over."

That then was why Virgil Calhoun could ride in so boldly. He had not even been seen by anyone except the home guard group, anxious to believe whatever its eyes beheld. The Southern Captain halted when the sleigh reached the door of a shuttered building bearing a sign, barely readable by starlight, "CRITERION SALOON." He turned Price over to the two troopers behind him, stepped down and walked back to the girls. The robes were removed, their ankles untied, they were helped to the sidewalk. Calhoun freed Sue Steelman's wrists and took out her gag. Price heard a resounding slap as she struck the Southerner's face, and then heard her high, indignant cry.

"Sir, I have never been so insulted. You are *no* gentleman."

It rang through the street but drew no attention. Calhoun caught both her hands in one of his, clapped his other across her mouth and told her firmly,

"It was only for your safety, Sue. These are dangerous

times. Now go along with the boys and you'll be well taken care of."

She flounced back, jerked free, turned on a toe and marched between two escorts through the door they held for her, a solid, curtained door in this climate. Ann was led after her.

Jack Price was unbound and dismounted, the gag left in place until he should be off the street. Calhoun turned the detail over to his lieutenant, nodded Price toward the door and followed him through it.

The room was brightly lighted by crystal chandeliers, making them pause while their eyes adjusted. When he could see, Price found some twenty men in city clothes at the bar and tables, dominated by a large, handsome figure with flowing mustaches. He was already on his way forward, both hands extended to clasp Calhoun's warmly, a white smile creasing his cheeks.

"Welcome back, Virgil. How was the sortie? Any trouble for you?" His deep voice had the soft slur of Virginia.

"None at all, Harrison. We ran into Allan Smith and some home guard coming in. They were very glad to see us."

"That jackass." The smile held. "Sometime I'll have a few drinks and kill him."

Jack Price would learn later about Charles Harrison. When he was sober there was no man more courtly, but drunk he would kill casually and without qualm. The bold eyes flicked over Price, then back to Calhoun.

"Two lovely ladies preceded you here. I assumed they

are your guests and required a room, which I provided. Are they friends?"

Virgil Calhoun shook with silent laughter. "The fair one is Miss Sue Steelman, the Union General's only daughter, a coquette. Not political. The other, Ann Ryan, a staunch Northerner, whose father was Overland station master at Julesburg when it was overrun by Indians."

Harrison's brows rose quizzically. "And this gentleman?"

"Captain Jack Price of the Union Army on detached duty out of uniform. Under orders to run down a rumor that Southerners posing as redskins are attacking the stations and coaches."

"Really?" The tone was ironic, then changed to quick hospitality. "But let us go through to my office and exchange news."

The long stride led them down the bar and into a comfortably appointed room at the rear. Jack Price understood that shouting to the customers would bring only laughter, for this would be a Southern cell, a gathering place for rebel sympathizers only. He could only wait, stay alert, and watch for opportunity that might be long in coming.

With the door closed on the bar Harrison set out fine whiskey in cut glassware and expensive cigars, waving toward chairs with velvet seats.

Sitting down, pouring, he looked at Price, still smiling. "You were at Julesburg, Captain? Virgil found you there?"

Price said tonelessly, "I was there. That was a genuine attack by a thousand or more red men." He took his whiskey in a long, slow swallow.

"Oh? So many? Tell me about it."

There was no reason not to and Jack Price relished what he had to say. He looked squarely at the man.

"Captain Calhoun destroyed Big Spring station and massacred eight men. Scalped them." A corner of his lip turned up. "He missed finding Miss Steelman there or she would probably not be alive now. A detail found her and took us to Julesburg, those who survived the Indians. Julesburg had evacuated. Only the Ryans stayed. They, I, a sergeant and two troopers got out in a blizzard to Fort Sedgwick. Calhoun had taken that. He brought us on."

"The other men, where are they?"

Price's eyes remained steady. "Calhoun abandoned them afoot at Sterling."

Harrison refilled his glass without speaking. Price tossed off the drink to cauterize the foul taste of the words. The Southern Captain's face had hardened during the recital, become defensive.

"I left them guns and lead."

Price did not pursue the matter. Harrison shrugged, drank, filled his and Price's glasses once more, and turned his attention to Calhoun.

"Let's save your report for the time being, but I must tell you of the changes here. We have a new governor." He offered his hands palms up in delight. "Gilpin. A Yankee but he's done us a fine turn. His first official act was to raise two companies of volunteers for the Union Army and pack them off. That leaves the defense of this territory up to the citizen soldiers and the Vigilantes. Virgil, what arms and ammunition they have when they're not patrolling they store in Baker's warehouse. You can destroy it all and when our Texans get here we can take over without a fight."

Harrison and Calhoun drank solemnly to the Governor. Jack Price did not touch his glass this time. Harrison's last phrases had come to his ears through an echo chamber. His head swam. At first he thought it was the impact of whiskey on a very weary body. Then as he slumped across the polished table he knew he had been drugged. His last awareness was of the Southerners' joined laughter.

CHAPTER NINE

Jack Price slept around the clock and more, half the time unconscious from whatever Charles Harrison had added to his whiskey, the remaining hours in the sleep of exhaustion. The long cross-country trip on the coaches topped by the flight from Big Spring, Julesburg, then the trek from Fort Sedgwick had compounded to sap almost the last of his endurance. When he waked the effects of the drug had worn off and his strength was largely restored. Except for a fog that clouded his mind so that he thought slowly and with effort, he felt refreshed.

Trying to clear his head, he reviewed the last day he remembered from the time the detail had come into Denver. He wondered how long ago that had been. Surely he could not be so rested in a period since he had passed out and a time when it was still dark. There had to be at least one day between. He thought of Ann Ryan and Sue Steelman, less concerned with their well being than their whereabouts. Virgil Calhoun had a heritage of gallantry to women and so must Harrison. Price believed they could be trusted to treat the girls with care and courtesy and make them comfortable.

And where was he himself? Lying on a pile of fur robes in a large room where a lamp burned low on top of a sealed hogshead. There were no windows in the walls. Barrels, crates, bales of soft goods were stacked against those. A skylight in the center of the ceiling, raised a fraction to admit air, showed darkness above it. A loft then.

Who had brought him here? Not Virgil Calhoun. The Captain would not have been so careless as to leave that avenue of escape over his head. Unless it was deliberate.

So far either Sue Steelman's opinion of Calhoun had restrained him from killing Price as he had the Union soldiers at Sedgwick, or Calhoun wanted him alive to trade for some Southerner prisoner of the North. If the second possibility was true the open skylight was someone's blunder. If it was Sue's influence the invitation to climb out of the loft was an invitation to be shot in escaping, for which Calhoun would not be held responsible by the blonde. There would be someone on the roof with a gun.

It was a long, methodical, step-by-step deliberation for Jack Price's slowly clearing brain to arrive at all these conclusions. When they were in order he knew that he must test them. This could be the first break for him. It could be the last.

He got up, walking around the floor until he was sure of his balance and muscle control, then, hauling crates beneath the skylight, he built a pyramid, saving those he found empty for the higher levels. Although his wounded shoulder was healed, lifting the crates sent twinges through it. He made more noise than he liked, sounds that would alert anyone waiting on the roof.

He stacked the boxes to within three feet of the light, climbed them and eased the window up a little to learn if it were free or rusted at the original angle. It lifted with a small creak. Satisfied, he returned to the floor, left the lamp burning because the glow did not reach the ceiling, picked up the bale of furs he had slept on and carried it with him, crouching on top of the pyramid.

Setting his feet firmly he filled his lungs, counted deliberately to five, held the furs over his head and straightened in a surge. The window flapped back, breaking the glass. He flung the fur bundle after it, high, twisted his body and rolled through the skylight, keeping flat against the roof.

A shot flashed from behind a chimney, aimed at the dark mass that fell on the window. Price waited without moving. A minute passed, then against the sky a darker shape separated itself from the chimney to move confidently to the broken window, fire a second shot into the black bulk of fur. Price saw an arm bend as the man shoved a gun into his holster, saw the figure kneel. Price jumped, cleared the skylight, landed on the man's back, was lucky in wrapping a choking grip around his neck. His momentum knocked the man flat. Price twisted, heaving on the neck, threw the man across his body and slammed the head against the roof. The man went limp.

Price snagged the gun from the holster, shoved it in his belt, and without ceremony rolled the figure through the skylight. The knock on the head had not been enough to kill, nor would the fall down the crates. They should be enough to keep the man out, unable to raise a cry until Price was well gone. He looked down and saw a sprawled blue uniform, one leg bending, then straightening in slow convulsions.

It was time to get off the roof. The two shots cracking across the silent town would bring Virgil Calhoun on the run and Price could not afford to be caught again. The rear edge was twenty feet away and he sprinted to it, bent forward trying to see what lay in the dark below. There was starlight enough to show a surface two stories down protruding from the back of the building a shade grayer than the black around it, a shed roof, he judged, perhaps seven feet wide. He lowered himself feet first, clinging to the edge until he hung full length, then let go and dropped. It was a hard fall, a hard landing. The sloping awning he hit was wood. A board broke and one leg jammed through it, a splinter cutting a gash above his knee. With a wrench of desperation he tore the splinter away, wincing at the pain, dragged the leg free and jumped blindly for the ground. He crashed in an open barrel of empty bottles that shattered under his boots, made a considerable racket, tipped the barrel over trying to climb out, lost the gun in his scramble and spent precious minutes fumbling over the sandy soil, expecting every second to hear boots running toward him.

None came. He found the gun, kept it in his hand and walked cautiously through the dark, his other hand feeling along the building until he reached a corner and turned that and immediately stumbled on a raised wooden sidewalk. It too had a wooden awning that threw the walk into black shadow.

Price did not know where he was, what street he was on, what direction it ran in. But there were no sounds and he had to move, to orient himself. He followed the sidewalk

to a second corner and from there saw a wide street crossing the narrower one he was on, more visible in the dim
starshine. He stepped into that. Abruptly, six feet from
him, a door opened, light flooded out and Jack Price
looked into the Criterion Saloon.

He felt his neck hairs rise. A man came out unsteady on
his feet, aimed himself toward Price and weaved past him.
Only because he was blinded by the dark after the bright
room did he not see the figure frozen against the wall. The
man fell off the sidewalk at the cross street, picked himself
up, slapped at his clothes and shambled on.

Price let his breath seep out, jumped to the dusty road
where his boots would not echo, and ran.

Calhoun's detail had ridden in on Larimer from the direction Price headed and the home guard men might still
be watching the road where they had met. They were the
only people he dared ask for information. At least Allan
Smith had wanted him hanged when he thought the prisoner was Southern and should be safe. If he could find the
man. Since the volunteers were the only defense in the city
against Indians there were probably Southerners among
them, and if he questioned one of those he would raise suspicion.

He was out of breath when he passed the last buildings
and saw the cluster of dark figures around the small fire at
the side of the road. He stopped to recover it so they would
not know he had been running, then walked forward.
When they had seen him before he had worn a hat and
heavy coat and been gagged, so they should not recognize

him without those things. Forty feet from them he stopped
again and called.

"Allan Smith there?"

An answer came. "I'm here. Who are you?"

"Come out here. I don't want to shout it."

There was a brief conference, then Smith detached himself from the others and walked cautiously toward Price,
his rifle raised.

"What are you doing outdoors after curfew?"

"I have a dispatch for Governor Gilpin. I don't know
where to find him."

"Who says? Who's it from?"

Jack Price supposed that the unsettled times and the Indian fright made everyone suspicious of strangers, and
there was no longer need to hide his identity.

"Captain Price, United States Army, on detached duty
from Washington. It is urgent that I see the Governor."

The man chewed his mustache, suspicious. "So urgent
you're out here without a horse and don't know where
you're going?"

"Mr. Smith," Price was sharp, "there is no time to argue
here and I can't explain further until I talk with Gilpin.
Tell me where he is and you'll hear more later."

"Well . . . he's got protection so I guess it'll be all right.
I'll show you his house."

He jogged back to the group to say he had to leave for a
while, then rejoined Price and led him through the dark
streets to one of the few brick residences set in a fenced
yard. Smith pointed it out from the corner, then hurried

back to his post. Price opened the gate and strode up the walk.

"Halt." The voice came out of the shadowed porch. "Who's there?"

"Captain Price to see Governor Gilpin." Price did not pause.

He climbed the steps but at the top the guard came away from beside the door, jamming a rifle in Price's stomach, his voice suddenly loud.

"That's no uniform, damn it. What's going on here?"

Price explained again, rapidly, but the guard did not move and his voice stayed high.

"You'd better have some proof to back that up or you'll get a belly full of lead."

Price hesitated, debating whether he could twist away before the trigger was pulled, grab the gun and club the man with it, but in the short pause the door opened, framing a man.

"What's the difficulty, Hays?"

Without relaxing a fraction the guard said, "Something suspicious here, Governor. I don't believe this bird that's trying to get to you. You'd best stay inside . . ."

Price interrupted hurriedly. "I have the proof he wants, sir. I'll show it to you inside. I must talk to you."

Gilpin was not a large man and was feeling the pressures that surrounded him, needing all the information he could hear. He did not hesitate but stood back from the door saying, "Let him pass, Hays. Come in, mister . . ."

"Captain, sir, Jack Price."

The guard lowered the gun reluctantly and moved

aside. Price stepped past him, followed the Governor into a lighted room where another man stood, a revolver in his hand. This one was tall, broad-shouldered, elegant in his long coat and vest. Gilpin closed the door, saying, "Well, Captain?"

"My report should be made to you alone, Governor."

"Whatever you have to say Tom Evans may hear. He is my closest adviser and the leader of our civilian defense."

Jack Price was uneasy about Evans but he saw no choice if he was to warn Gilpin. He said, "There is a detail of troopers in town wearing Union blue, but they are Confederates under Captain Virgil Calhoun. They captured Fort Sedgwick, took me prisoner, stole the uniforms and blew up the fort before coming here."

Both men looked at each other as if Price were mad. Gilpin said explosively, "Impossible. While Colonel Chivington is in the mountains recruiting and since his arrival the Captain is the ranking officer in Denver. He commands our military installation here and the men Chivington will send down."

"Confederate officer, Governor. Not Union." Jack Price had the sensation of everything inside him sinking. It was unthinkable that the largest city in the territory should be under Southern control, worse that it was so by hoax.

Gilpin's face had turned pale, his voice faint. "I cannot believe what you say."

"Neither can I." Tom Evans shook a thick forefinger at Price. "I don't know who you are or what your game is but you won't get by with it. Who do you pretend to be anyway?"

"John Price, Captain, Army of the Potomac on detached duty."

Evans brows climbed. "Do you have any proof of that wild statement?"

"If I may sit down." When Gilpin nodded Price took a chair, worked off his left boot, peeled back the soft lining, drew out a paper and held it up.

The Governor took it as if it might bite, read it and in silence passed it to Evans. The home guard leader was longer in reading, then lifted his eyes to examine Price more closely and slowly returned the document to him. No one spoke until the paper was back in its place, the boot on the foot again and Price had stood up. Gilpin looked at Evans as though he would not commit himself without the agreement of the other.

Evans was slow in his speech. "It appears to be in order. Unless it is forged. If you were really held prisoner how did you get here?"

"Calhoun set a trap to have me shot escaping. I sprung it, got away and found a guide to bring me."

"Maybe. What are you doing in Colorado out of uniform? On what duty?"

Price explained. "Big Ben Holladay insisted to President Lincoln that Southerns masquerading as Indians were destroying his stations. General Curtis sent me to find out the truth."

"And you found out?"

Price was grim. "I found out. Virgil Calhoun's detail murdered eight men at Big Spring station."

Gilpin sank into the chair Price had vacated, gray faced. "How did you learn that?"

"I tricked him into a confession."

"How did you know the men at Sedgwick were Southern?"

"Calhoun and I attended school at the Point together. He's from the South and I had heard that he along with many others had followed Lee into the rebel army."

Gilpin drew his hand down his face to loosen its tightness. "Intolerable." His agonized eyes lifted to Evans. "Tom, I have turned over what recruits Chivington has sent to the man. What a dreadful situation."

Price told him, "It will worsen unless you take quick action. The Southerns intend to seize the arms in the warehouse. A brigade of three thousand Texans is coming from New Mexico. Reinforced by them, Calhoun can take the entire territory. He has already disorganized the Overland. He wants the gold and silver from the camps because the Confederacy is so short of foreign exchange. As you know, when the war began they depended on their cotton crops to trade with France and England for arms, but our blockade has kept most of their shipping from getting through."

Gilpin sounded stunned into helplessness, looking to Evans for support. "I don't know what to do, Tom, where to start."

"First," Price said, "get a wire through to General Curtis detailing the information I have given you."

"Yes," Evans agreed. "But as shaken as we both are you

had better send the wire yourself to be sure it's complete. I'll take you to the telegraph office."

"Thank you, Tom." Gilpin sagged against the chair, his breathing slow and heavy. "When you finish there bring the Captain back here. He'll be safer and he can help us plan a course of action."

CHAPTER TEN

Tom Evans set a brisk pace toward the business section, saying as they turned the first corner, "You say Calhoun set a trap and you sprung it empty. I'd be interested to hear about it."

Price told how he had escaped and the home guard man made a wordless growl, then said, "I heard the shots. They came from near the Criterion but by the time my men got there everything was quiet. Harrison said the disturbance had been in the street and he had not investigated because he assumed it was one of our patrols and didn't want to be caught out during curfew."

"Mr. Harrison," Price said sharply, "is up to his neck in the Copperhead movement. He should be arrested immediately."

Evans started, paused, then walked on, his voice grim. "Right now we don't have the manpower for both Indian fighting and a fight with Calhoun's people if we should try to arrest him. You see, we know there are Southerns in the home guard and they could be expected to take that side. We'll have to wait for more of Chivington's recruits."

They said no more until they reached a brick building on Larimer at Sixteenth, where Evans stopped and tried the door. It was not locked and he pushed it inward, went through to a dark room with Price behind him and stopped.

"Wait here. I'll go bring the operator. Don't make a light because the window isn't curtained. I won't be long."

Evans backed out and closed the door. It was ink black in the room, giving Price a claustrophobic sensation. To get rid of that, he felt his way along the wall, came against a chair, went around that and hit a desk. Running his hands over it he touched a box with matches in it and risked lighting one, cupping it in his hands long enough to see where he was.

It was an office with a wooden cabinet but no other furniture. The desk held a stack of clean papers, a pen and inkpot. That was all. No telegraph key. No wires. It had struck Price as strange that the operator should have gone off and left the door unlocked, and the bare room was stranger still. Not by nature a suspicious person, since Fort Sedgwick he had considered any oddity more closely than he normally would. Now he had second thoughts about Tom Evans. The home guard man had given no indication of being other than Gilpin had claimed, but why had he brought Price here to a place that was certainly not a telegraph office?

He dropped the match, took the gun from his belt and by feel found three unspent bullets in it. With it in his hand he started for the door but stopped short at the tramp of boots on the walk outside and turned back. The brief match flare had reflected off a rear window though there was no door there. He ran, shoved the sash up, jumped through onto ground three feet below and closed the sash, crouched beneath it to listen. The front door was thrown open and the glow of a lantern filled the room. Tom Evans' voice cursed.

Virgil Calhoun's voice bit at him. "Why didn't you get rid of him while you had the chance?"

"I wanted him alive to learn what else he knows and may have blabbed about to somebody. Never mind, he can't have got far by this time. Let's find him."

The lantern light went out as the door closed behind them. There had been more than two men on the walk but Price did not know how many. He did not know which way their search would go first, or if it would split in opposite directions. But he could not stay here in the alley, for it would be one of the first places they would look. The only safety might be in the dark office, where they would probably not come again.

He raised the sash, climbed through and closed it, crouching beside the window, holding the gun with its half-filled chamber that would not be enough to help much if he needed it.

He saw the lantern brought into the alley at the left end, then heard the angry murmur of voices, Calhoun's peremptory tone still blaming the home guard man. Then the glow and sounds faded as the search passed the window.

Price stayed where he was. He did not know how long they would look for him but he allowed an hour for them to move out of the area. He would have to get back to the Governor but he suspected Calhoun and Evans would stake the house out as a first precaution against his return there.

For all he knew Gilpin himself could have Southern sympathies. Harrison had said his first act had been to send the Union troops east. Had he done so to clear the area, leave it open to the rebels under the guise of a patriotic gesture? But the way the man had reacted to Price's report had appeared genuine shock, and there was no other authority he could reach in time to prevent a takeover of the city at least. Fort Morgan was too far away. Gilpin might have understood Tom Evans' intention when he sent them off together, might fire on him at a second visit, but he must take that chance.

When he moved he left by the window. A moon had risen low in the east but it slipped in and out of clouds. Choosing the times when it was hidden, Price took a different route than Evans had brought him, coming up to the street a block away from the house at a corner beyond the one he had turned before. A frame residence there sat back in an unfenced yard. Price turned in against it short of the corner, kept close to the wall until he could see the Governor's yard in the middle of the block across the street. He waited there, wanting the moon now, and when it came he made out two dark lumps behind Gilpin's picket fence near the gate. He was about to retreat, detour further and come in from the rear when a match was struck, a cigarette lighted, all the proof needed of an ambush. Price wondered what the guard Hays had been told. And if there was a guard behind the house who would be a problem.

He made a wide sweep until he could see the kitchen porch and stopped in deep shadow to reconnoiter. There was no roof over the small platform and another shaft of moonlight showed him a figure in front of the door. Price did not want another confrontation, sounds that could bring Calhoun's watchdogs running.

He backed off again, paralleled the side fence and studied the windows. Moonbeams winked off window glass, a row of six with a gap near the middle where the lower pane was open. Price lay down, worked his way to the fence and when another cloud crossed the moon stepped over the pickets and dropped flat again. There had been no sign of a dog earlier and there was none as he crawled on elbows and thighs to the wall and lay against that while another moment of light passed. Then he went through the window fast.

He was in a dark bedroom, a streak of light at the bottom of the door. The dog was there, a small animal that set up a hysteric yapping. Price grabbed for it, picked it up and held its jaws together, moving toward the door. Before he reached it, it opened and Gilpin was in the hall with a table lamp and a forty-five.

"Ginger, what is it? Who's in there?"

Price whirled aside into darkness, saying quickly, "Captain Price. Don't put the light on me. Are you alone?"

The Governor backed away, rattled. "I'm alone. What are you doing here?"

"I'll tell you in the study. Blow out the hall lamp so I won't be seen from outside."

"You gave me a start."

Gilpin kept backing to the bracket lamp against the wall, turned the wick down and retreated to the study at the front of the house. Price tossed the dog at the bed, went through the doorway, pulled the panel closed and followed the glow that came through the open study door. Gilpin was just setting the table lamp down as Price paused to be sure the curtains were still pulled before he entered the bright room. The Governor froze, staring.

"What in the name of God happened to you?"

Price crossed to stand before the Governor. He saw now what had caused Gilpin's shocked question, the thick sand down the length of his clothes, collected as he crawled.

He stood very still so no more than had already would fall. "If you've got a newspaper to stand on I'll brush off while I talk." While Gilpin spread a paper from the desk Price told him, "Your Tom Evans is a traitor. Instead of a telegraph office he took me somewhere, left me in the dark saying he'd bring the operator. What he brought was Virgil Calhoun and a squad to take me. I suspected and left before they came, waited outside the window and heard Calhoun damn Evans for not killing me, heard Evans say he wanted to grill me to see who else I'd talked to."

"Tom Evans?" It was a harsh gasp. "It can't be true."

"It is true. They're looking for me and there are two of them in your yard to waylay me. Go ask your sentry out front."

Gilpin chewed his lip, the pupils of his eyes wide and dark on Price, then he started toward the entrance. Price moved behind the door as it was opened, out of sight.

"Hays," the Governor almost whispered, "are there two men in this yard who shouldn't be here?"

"It's all right, Governor." The guard was soothing. "Mr.

Evans posted them for added protection because the patrols say a crazy man is on the loose, threatening you."

Gilpin groaned, then raised his voice, shouting. "You two, get out of this yard or I'll have you shot. When I want Tom Evans' protection I'll ask for it. Clear off."

A shout came back. "We have to follow orders, Governor, for your own good."

"My orders supersede any others. I tell you to leave."

The two figures stood up, uncertain, and walked reluctantly away. Gilpin told Hays waspishly, "If they come back or you see others fire a warning shot and if they move closer aim to hit."

He stepped inside and closed the door in a slow, deliberate swing that ended in a firm click of the catch. It sounded to Price like a knell to the Governor's doubt. Gilpin leaned against the jamb, keeping hold of the knob, looking at the floor.

His voice when it came was dull. "Captain, I don't know what to think. Tom Evans was one of the Committee of Ten, the Vigilante group which so effectively cleared out the toughs here earlier. A brave band they were."

"There is courage on both sides, Governor. The rest of the Committee, are you sure any of them are loyal?"

Gilpin raised haunted eyes, a bitter twist to his lips. "I think so, but until ten minutes ago I'd have sworn by Evans. All I can say is that five of them come from the Northeast states."

"You're going to need their help right away. Calhoun is going after the arms stored for the home guard and recruits. I'd guess the only reason he hasn't reached for them yet is that he doesn't want to expose his hand until the Texans come and there's no telling how close they are."

"Not very. If they were near I'd have had word from the south. But we shouldn't gamble on a guess about Calhoun. With you still free he may move right away." Gilpin shook himself out of the lethargy the unmasking of Evans had wrapped him in, and straightened with decision. "I'll go round up the boys and we can move the arsenal tonight. You wait here. I'll turn out the lamp as if I've gone to bed."

Price pulled the gun from his belt. "Before you leave, have you any ammunition for this in case Evans comes here?"

"Oh. Yes."

Gilpin carried the lamp into another room, returned shortly with a box of forty-five shells, a Greening shotgun and charges of buckshot for that, turned out the lamp and left the house.

Price sank into the deep leather chair beside the desk and in its comfort the temptation was great to sleep. The hours of tension were draining him. But he did not dare. If Evans did come, the guard Hays would pass him in without question. He waited an hour before boots crossed the porch, several pairs, and he leveled the Greening on the door. It opened, men came into the dark room, then it closed.

Gilpin's voice said, "Captain? Are you awake?"

"Yes." Price let out his held breath and lowered the gun. "I'll make a light."

CHAPTER ELEVEN

The lamp's glow spread over the Governor and five men behind him. Price looked from one to another quickly, his first impression approving. They were young, twenty to twenty-five, the age group that was settling the frontier. This was not an old man's country. They were straight and strong looking, their eyes direct on him. They were armed with short guns and rifles and the butts were worn to a glossy patina.

Gilpin introduced them by code names, saying the Vigilantes kept their identities secret except from each other.

He continued, "Gentlemen, meet Captain Jack Price of the Union Army. Captain, these men are here without knowing why. They asked no questions. I want them to hear from you yourself what trouble we are in."

Price talked and no one interrupted. Their expressions changed as each new fact came out, skeptical at first, alert for any hole in the recital, finally dark with anger, but he had to show his credentials again before they fully believed.

They kept silent after he finished, digesting what they had heard, then a tall redhead with a nasal New England twang spoke rapidly.

"The Vigilance headquarters. We can move the magazine before daylight and nobody the wiser, pull enough boys off guard duty to fort up there and hold it."

"Good place, Codfish." It was Gilpin.

"Let's move. Everybody go for a wagon and we meet at the warehouse."

Codfish was on his way when the Governor said, "I'll be along as soon as I get my rifle."

Price raised a hand to him. "You're not going, sir."

The Governor bridled. "You don't give me orders."

"Think about it yourself, sir. You are the legal chief of government in this territory. If something happened to you the Southerners would have a field day."

"He's right, Governor." The redhead was firm. "We're expendable if it comes to that, but you're the only man with a chance of holding the city for the Union."

Gilpin accepted the judgment with no more argument and the rest left. They separated at the street, heading for different liveries. The redhead took Price in tow, giving a rundown on the warehouse armory.

Before the outbreak of hostilities it had belonged to the militia company, but those fighting men were long gone, called to the war in the east. The building had been commandeered by the home guard that had been hastily raised when the militia left and the danger of attack from the Plains tribes loomed after Sand Creek. When Codfish and Price rolled up before it, it was a long, one-story frame structure with narrow, empty lots on either side, flanked by similar buildings.

Codfish had no key but the lock broke when he hit it several times with the butt of his short gun. The four other men arrived with wagons before the door was opened and they filed into a barn of a place where the guardsmen had drilled in bad weather.

Now the rear was crowded with stacks of guns, boxes of assorted ammunition, forty-five shells, Minie balls, chests of powder, and cases of copper percussion caps. Price's experienced eye measured the volume of material and he judged that Gilpin and Chivington had amassed enough to equip a regiment. It was disappointing that the weapons were not more modern, but then those the Southerners had were no better.

It would take precious time to load all of it and Price's tension doubled. Gilpin had put his finger on the need for haste in saying that with Price escaped Virgil Calhoun would probably try to capture this place right away. Right away tonight. And if he brought his detail while they were working here, five Vigilantes and one captain were too few to stand them off.

They set up a line down the room, Price at the deep end, passing articles from man to man at a run, the one at the front throwing what he received in the wagon drawn close to the door. That was the slower job and guns, boxes were piled at the entrance. When the rear was emptied everyone would turn to loading.

The night was waning, the darker hour just before dawn approaching, and they raced against it. A lighted lantern set midway of the floor let them see dimly what they were doing but they were a ghostly crew.

One wagon was filled and replaced at the door. The pile there was high. Codfish called a halt in the transfer chain, called the men up the room to move it to the wagon and make room for more. Price had started forward when guns hammered from outside.

He saw the lead horse of the second wagon fall and entangle the team. Then the men began dropping, picked out by the lantern. There was nothing he could do to help. From where he stood he could see nothing to shoot at, not even muzzle flashes.

In seconds all of the Vigilantes were down and the last to drop sprawled against the lantern, his foot breaking it. There was a moment of blackness then flame swirled up from spilled oil. The lantern rolled, dribbling, leaving a trail that the flame followed immediately. It crashed against a powder keg spewing oil over that and flame licked up the wood.

Jack Price ran for the rear entrance. He could not help the Union by dying here. Yells came to him, Calhoun bawling to get the loaded wagon away. They were too long at moving it. The powder exploded, blasted out the front wall, threw flaming debris onto the explosives in the wagon and that blew apart. The terrified team bolted, scattering flame behind.

Price saw none of that. He reached the rear door, yanked it open, looked back once to see the front wall a seething fire, then dived outside. It was still dark there and he ran across the narrow lot for shelter behind the next building, catching a glimpse of Calhoun's men driving down the street away from further explosions.

He could not stay where he was. Already the building that hid him was crackling and would soon drive him into the open where he could be spotted if Calhoun stayed in the area. Then in a rush the streets around him were filled with hurrying men. The curfew was forgotten. People in the Western towns feared fire as much as Indians. It had totally destroyed many of the sun-dried wood communities.

A hose wagon manned by volunteers was dragged to the vacant lot, leather hose stretched and the pumpers worked in rhythm, the leader bawling orders through a leather trumpet. Price went around the building to the street. No one glanced at him, the crowd too intent on fighting the flames. He moved through it away from the blazing light that filled the sky. Walls and roofs collapsed behind him, thundering down. Even when he reached Gilpin's street the red glow threw the neighboring houses into sharp black silhouette.

Both Hays and the Governor were on the porch, Gilpin calling anxiously as Price came through the gate, asking what the fire was. Price said nothing until they were indoors alone, then he reported. Gilpin clasped hands together hard against his chest.

"Those fine boys. What a loss. Damn Calhoun. And even if he didn't get the arms he wins. They're lost to us. How can we fight him?"

"The miners must have side arms and rifles in the mountains. We'll have to contact Chivington, warn him. Where is he?"

Gilpin poured brandy for them, drank two himself to dull his shock before he answered. "The last word I had he intended to go to Central City. Whether he's been there and left I don't know."

"It's a starting place. Where is it?"

The Governor turned to a map against the wall, traced a road with a finger, a tortuous winding climb to the camp.

"It's a hard, cold ride, Captain, and you look near exhaustion. A few hours now can't set us back farther than we are, but we would indeed be ruined if you fell by the trail. You are to lay over here until tomorrow night. While you sleep I'll get together an outfit for you, coat, hat, gloves, fresh trousers, traveling gear. Have something to eat now, then take the spare bedroom. And stay in it unless I come for you. There's no telling who may come by."

There was good reason in all the Governor said. Price ate in the kitchen and hardly knew when he climbed between the sheets. He slept deeply until the next noon, when Gilpin knocked softly on the door and came in at Price's answer.

Gilpin was grimly smug. "Tom Evans just left," he said. "He came asking if I had seen you, said you'd disappeared while he was waking up the telegraph officer. I can lie as well as any politician so I worried that you had fallen into Calhoun's hands." He used a sardonic smile. "We were both convincing. Are you rested?"

Price said he was, dressed in the clothes the Governor had brought, then rejoined the man in the kitchen for a noon meal. Gilpin had made it himself, had sent his manservant away so he would not know there was a guest.

They spent the afternoon talking and writing. A telegram to General Curtis that Gilpin would send by special messenger to be forwarded from Fort Morgan. Credentials for Price to present to Chivington when he found him. Price asked that Gilpin quietly try to learn where the two girls were being kept, not to move them but to tell Ann Ryan privately that Jack Price was alive and free, cautioning that Sue Steelman was not to hear of that since she was an unknown quantity.

After full dark they went to the barn behind the house where Gilpin had a strong, big-chested black horse waiting. While Price saddled it, loaded on bedroll and equipment, and shoved a new rifle into the boot, the Governor gave him last instructions.

"In Central City look up Wilkes De Frees. I'd send you to John Gregory but he hails from Georgia and I feel entitled to suspect even him now. De Frees is from northern Indiana and should be safe. He'll know where Chivington is." In the lantern light he looked deep into Price's face, offering a hand. "A safe passage, Captain. Colorado hangs by a thread in your hands."

As Gilpin had planned Price rode out toward Fort Morgan with a messenger's pass to take him through the patrol, and then swung around to the west. The road was hard packed, in good condition because of the heavy traffic between Denver and the mountain camps of Central City, Black Hawk, and Idaho Springs. The freighters and stagecoach people pitched in to maintain it year round. Although the winter was hard and spring came late to the higher elevations, the way was cleared of the last blizzard, narrow but passable.

At daylight he pulled off the winding track in a turnout

where wagons could get by each other, built a fire of dead-fall, hobbled the black to rest from the climb, made coffee and laced it with Taos dynamite, a thoughtful addition of Gilpin's. He ate a little, rolled in his blanket and slept for two hours.

The rattle of chain harness on a six-horse team waked him and he turned uphill again through deep snowbanks on either side, grateful for the heavy coat and gloves. It was night again when he brought the tired horse up through Russell Gulch and into the busy camp.

Part of his afternoon talk with Gilpin had been given to a briefing on the area history. Central City was now the largest of the settlements, established by John Gregory of Georgia, come west to look for gold and finding it after a number of attempts.

Two of his home state neighbors had fired his enthusiasm when they returned from a trek to the California gold fields in the early fifties, disappointed that all the good ground had already been staked out but eager to try again in the new Colorado strike. The Russell brothers made up a company to go west, but Gregory, broke in the depression, set out alone, working his way. He made it as far as Laramie, pausing there to drive a team to build a stake for the next lap.

In '58 news reached Gregory that the Russells had found gold to the south at the juncture of Cherry Creek and the Platte River. He headed for the strike on foot and reached Auraria in late March, only to learn that the creek was a bust and the Russells had headed east for more men to come back and search the hills for the lode from which the tantalizing flakes in the little stream had come.

Redheaded and impatient John Gregory headed for the mountains at once although it was still early spring. His impetuosity almost cost him his life in a three-day blizzard. But surviving that, he did make a rich find and with friends who grub-staked him to develop it organized the Gregory Mining District in '59. The code they laid down to govern themselves became the basic mining law for the new territory of Colorado.

The early settlements that sprung up around such finds called themselves by such names as Gregory Diggings, Russell Diggings and the like, but as they expanded they changed to pomposity, such as Mountain City. Camped one night where Eureka, Nevada and Gregory creeks join, the redhead John Gregory observed over two miles of campfires. He decided the time had come that the area deserved to become Central City, and so the whole combination of gulches was renamed.

It had long passed the boom camp stage when Captain Jack Price rode the black up muddy Eureka Street, stabled it at Pollock's livery and walked down Main, called by then Gamblers' Row because every other establishment was a saloon. Businesses and residences were no longer lodged in tents but solid wood structures and a few of brick. One of the latter was the Miners' Hotel and Price found a place there.

Signing the register, he asked the gangling clerk whether he knew if Colonel Chivington was in town, and learned that he was recruiting, probably that evening at the Roundhouse Saloon, so there was no need to risk Wilkes De Frees being a secret Southern sympathizer.

Price took his bedroll to the room before he returned to the street to find the Roundhouse. It was not late but the early February night had settled down and the chill wind had nearly emptied the road. Price's nose was red and weeping by the time he located the sign.

CHAPTER TWELVE

As a contrast to harried Denver, the high mountain camp blazed with lights from Gamblers' Row and merchants who stayed open to accommodate miners coming off the evening shifts. From the noisy exuberance in the saloons as Price passed they were all crowded. When he pushed through the door of the Roundhouse the roar was deafening and the heat from a stove and many bodies was stifling.

As the mines had exhausted the surface "blossom rock," easy to extract because of centuries of erosion, the veins twisted down through hard, unyielding strata more and more difficult to break through. The owners of the claims began importing Cornish miners from the Middle West, largely from Michigan, men with long experience in hard-rock. Now there were hundreds of them in Central City.

There was never a breed, including the Irish, who enjoyed jokes, practical or plain, and song as much as the Cousin Jacks. The Roundhouse rang with lusty voices of a crowd around a blue uniform at the center. Jack Price could just make out the bright shoulder straps of a colonel, singing with the rest. The swaying crush was good natured as he wedged through to the officer's side.

When the song ended in a shout of laughter Price

touched the blue elbow, raising his voice to be heard. "Speak to you, sir?"

Chivington's rather heavy face was flushed from the vocal exercise and drinking. His bold, arrogant eyes measured Price as if to estimate his worth as a fighting man.

"If you're here to volunteer, you may."

Price bent close to the man's ear so his words would not carry to the miners. "I have a message from Governor Gilpin."

Chivington's face turned haughty and hard. "Bothersome civilian. What's he want now?"

"I can't tell you in this madhouse but it is most important that you hear me at once and in private. Please come to the hotel."

"Now? But my man, I am busy looking for men."

"I'll help you look as soon as you know what's happening down the mountain. It is urgent."

The miners were singing again. Chivington did not want to leave them. He pulled at his lower lip for a long moment before deciding to go with this stranger.

"Very well, but make it short."

Jack Price shouldered a path to the door. Behind him the Colonel stopped on the sidewalk, saying brusquely, "Now, what is this message?"

Price had been through enough in the last days that his temper was on a short fuse. Impatience with this pompous officer rode him and he could crowd it down only far enough to keep his voice empty.

"It is rather longer than you'll want to stand in this cold listening to. The hotel is better."

Price walked away and after a moment the Colonel followed, caught up and kept pace without another word. In the hotel room Price lit the lamp, gave Chivington the only chair and sat on the bed working off his boot, extracting the credentials from the Army and Gilpin, handing them across.

"Captain John Price, Army of the Potomac reporting, sir."

Chivington swelled in hostility, demanding before he glanced at the papers, "Why are you out of uniform?"

"On detached duty for General Curtis, sent west to run down rumors that Southern guerrillas are raiding Overland stage stations, impersonating Indians. They are."

"Bosh." Chivington scanned the papers and flicked them back. "Is that what you dragged me here to claim?"

"It's true and there is a great deal more." Price talked rapidly trying to prevent interruption.

Chivington listened with stony skepticism and, to drive home to him the extent of the danger, Price saved the report of the Texas brigade until he had told all the rest. When he finished Chivington snorted a derisive laugh.

"Your Captain Calhoun may think he has Denver but we'll handle that in good time. As to this Texas scare, I am astonished that a Union officer would believe such a fabrication."

"Colonel, believe me, it is no fabrication."

"Bah. From the beginning of the war rumors have been flying that the Southerners will overrun the entire West.

They're going to take Santa Fe. They'll win Albuquerque. Then Tucson. They're starting the rumors themselves, using fright to demoralize the people. Do you expect me to believe three thousand Texans can march clear from Austin across the Texas plains through Comanche and Apache country, march three hundred miles to the Colorado line *and* then on to attack Denver?"

"I do. So does Calhoun. And you should."

Chivington filled his cheeks with air, blew it out. "Captain, it frightens me that such gullible men as you are commanding our troops. No wonder we're losing everything."

Price kept his head down, working at the boot he had pulled on again as if it were not properly on his foot. If he looked up the Colonel would see the fury in his eyes. When he could trust his voice he changed the subject, knowing he had made no impression on the obdurate man, knowing if anything was done Price would have to do it himself.

"Is the recruiting up here going well?"

"No." Chivington was sharp. "Who wants to volunteer into an army that is routed every time it takes the field?"

"Don't the miners understand that if the Confederates win Colorado their mines will be confiscated?"

"There's no use telling them that. They're more afraid of claim jumpers than of an army so far away."

"I said I'd help you. I'll talk to them. Let's go back to the saloons."

Chivington stood up with alacrity, saying sourly, "It's a free country but you might as well save your breath."

They left the hotel, walked through a rising raw wind

and Price stopped at the corner of Gamblers' Row. The Colonel started to pass on toward the Roundhouse but Price stepped in front of him.

"You'd better come in and introduce me, sir. They'll pay more attention than to someone they don't know."

Chivington went into the first saloon with him, disapproval plain in his stiff bearing as they worked to the bar through the well-filled room. Price separated a bill from the packet in his pocket, another thoughtful contribution from Gilpin, held it in front of the bartender.

"For this I want to write a notice on your mirror."

"What notice? Who the hell are you?"

Chivington clipped out, "Captain Price, Union Army. Out of uniform under orders. Give him a chalk." The Colonel about-faced and left.

"That's different, mate." The bartender's grin showed a gold tooth.

He exchanged a stub of chalk for the bill and went back to pouring whiskey while Price went around the bar, printing in large letters,

MASS MEETING
IN FRONT OF COURTHOUSE
NINE O'CLOCK TOMORROW MORNING.
IMPORTANT TO ATTEND.

There was a pause of curiosity as he wrote, then a man against the counter shouted above the noise around him, "What's it about, Doc?"

Price too shouted. "Confederates coming to take the mines. A lot of them. I'll explain at the meeting."

The sound level dropped, then picked up again, the tone changed from banter to questioning. Price leaned across the bar to the man who had asked the question, offered to stake him to drinks if he would make the rounds of the saloons and vouch for his identity, and did not have to urge him.

They moved from place to place leaving the trail of notices, reaching the last one after three in the morning. His guide was happily unsteady and the crowd there had been very thin but it did not matter. Bartenders down the line had told him the word had preceded him, as news spreads quickly through communities where entertainment is restricted and men must use their own resources against boredom.

The man behind this final counter said all Central City had heard of the call and couriers were already on their way to Idaho Springs, Black Hawk and the lesser camps. He would draw a crowd. They were given drinks on the house there, then Price left his guide to return to the hotel.

He had made a start, done the best he could think of and in the morning he would see if Chivington was right. An urgent excitement, a pressure kept him from resting well. He lay in the dark room that smelled of many previous occupants, churning over what he would say.

When he had left Washington his duty had seemed a simple one, to learn the truth of one rumor and report back to Curtis. Now he was in the middle of a far more ugly concern. Chivington obviously would take no action on his own and must be by-passed. It was squarely up to Captain Jack Price to raise an army to face the Texans. An army of miners, untrained in the military arts who would be the only defense against the drilled soldiers of the South.

Chivington was an enigma. Price did not understand this man who had led the Sand Creek massacre on a headstrong impulse instead of taking a more logical corrective action and now brushed off an immensely more formidable foe. He forced the puzzle out of his mind to sleep, to be ready for the next day's task.

The morning was clear and cold. Jack Price ate a heavy, hot breakfast for the inner warmth it would give, then walked to the courthouse at High Street and St. James, facing on Eureka. The throng that had gathered outdid anything he had imagined, spilling out of the main streets into the byways where they would not be able to hear a word, would have to rely on what the closer audience would relay back.

Price crushed through to the courthouse steps, climbed to the top looking in vain for Chivington, who should be here to support him but was not. A square, solid man handed him a fireman's trumpet, looking eager for a speech.

"Go to it, Jack. What's this about Johnny Reb grabbing our mines."

To convince these men, to make the talk as strong as possible, Price began with the Big Spring raid, played on the Fort Sedgwick deceit, the vulnerability of Denver with a Southern captain already commanding there. He shouted of his capture and escape, his time with Gilpin and his authority to raise a company here. Again he saved the Texas brigade until last, adding that Calhoun had taunted him with the plan to capture the mines for the South.

Until then the men had listened with the detached interest they would give a good barroom tale. They had not been much affected that Calhoun controlled Denver or that the home guard armory was destroyed. But a threat to the mines brought a strong reaction.

Most of them had fought all their lives for one reason or another. It was not cowardice that had kept them from volunteering, but as Chivington had said it was fear that if they left the mountains someone would jump their claims. The vision of the Southerners being the claim jumpers put the war in a wholly different light.

A growl spread like a wave outward from the courthouse. Noisy arguments rose here and there, three or four fights erupted where there were Southern sympathizers. Price used all his lung power through the horn.

"You men are needed to stop that take-over. There's no one else to do it. How many . . . ?"

He was interrupted by a miner just below him, a man with a bull voice that carried as far as Price's without amplification.

"Can we elect our own officers?"

The custom at that time allowed voluntary companies to choose their own leaders, and while Price would rather have held the command himself he knew that as a stranger he was not likely to be followed by any great number. If they rose to the call this would be a citizen army and the miltiary was not generally admired. Price did not hesitate.

"That's right."

The man ran up the steps to his side, bawling, "I'm in, boys, and I nominate Slough for Colonel. Step up, J.D., and lead off."

There was a pause for democracy to function, a wait for other nominations, but none was offered and there was no protest. J. D. Slough was chosen by unanimous consent. Price watched a man in the front ranks shove a way to the steps and mount them deliberately, a strong figure in a miner's red shirt who nodded at and then ignored Jack Price, turning to wait out a roared triple cheer. Then he raised both arms high for quiet.

Without preamble he rattled off a string of names. "You boys set up in the saloons and register a company. Tell the bartenders every volunteer is entitled to a free whiskey and cigars on me. Supply your own guns. That's all now."

Another cheer and a build of enthusiasm gathered momentum as the crowd dissolved toward their favorite bars. Price admired the man's directness and brevity, the show of good leadership. The miners knew what they were doing.

Slough faced Price then, held out a hand, showed white teeth in a wide smile. "Anything else I can do here, Captain?"

Price took the hand, returned the smile, sobered. "One thing. Where's Chivington? I expected him this morning."

A corner of the new civilian colonel's lip turned up. "He took the early stage for Denver. God knows why. That's one man I can't figure. You know him?"

"Met him last night. What about him?"

"He fought as a guerrilla with the jayhawkers in the

Kansas John Brown troubles before he drifted west. No sign of yellow then. He's a high elder in the Methodist church, brimstone-and-damnation preacher. Quotes the Bible faster than I can cuss. Maybe he hightailed for Denver to throw out your Johnny Rebs." He broke off, raising his voice. "Hey, Manuel, come up here." Then to Price again, "A man you ought to know."

A stocky, smooth-faced, olive-skinned man jumped the steps.

Slough introduced him. "Manuel Chavez, Captain Price. He's a New Mexican and knows the country like his hand. Manuel, I'm appointing you my lieutenant colonel as of now."

Chavez bowed with mock gravity. "Gracias for the honor, Señor Colonel Slough. Am I deserving?"

"Stow it, boy. I want you because you know that ground and I don't. Let's get out of this fresh air while you tell me where those Texans will start from."

Taking Price's and Chavez's arms, Slough went down the steps, angling toward the nearest saloon. Chavez was quiet until they were inside the warm room at a table. There with a wet glass in his hand he drew a liquid map trailing across the surface.

"El Paso, I think. Up the Rio Grande valley north to Albuquerque. If they take that town, on to Santa Fe. If they succeed there they swing east to Las Vegas then north again through Apache Canyon, Glorieta Pass to attack Fort Union. The Santa Fe trail that far. If they get beyond there they go to Raton Pass and come into

Colorado." His full lips twisted. "Denver must be much important. That is a long march."

"Colorado is important," Price put in. "The South is running out of gold and credit to pay for the war. I suppose your people will side with them?"

Chavez said hotly, "No. Not with Texans. Captain, that country the conquistadors made Spanish three hundred years ago. It is still Spanish. In the whole territory I think there are maybe a hundred Anglos besides the regular soldiers Colonel Canby has. The Texans will have no help. We have not forgotten those settlers stole our land and after the Mexican War tried to steal all New Mexico. Only the federal government stopped that, so we honor the Union. My father writes that many of our men have joined the Union militia to fight the Texans when they come."

Puzzled, Price asked, "In spite of our winning the war with Mexico?"

Chavez drew wet circles with his empty glass, looking into it, looking at history. "Captain, my people are not Mexican. We are *sangre azul*. Back for over two hundred years every family member is registered in the Corte de Purismo de Sangre . . . of purest blood . . . We do not like the Mexicans much but the Texans we hate."

While he listened Jack Price had kept one eye on the table where volunteers were signing up in impressive numbers and he felt a personal warmth for everyone. It did not matter that they were going out not for the sake of the government in Washington but to hold their own mines. Only professional soldiers ever fought for something other than their homes and way of life.

Slough had been patient through Chavez's talk, but now it was finished he had orders for his lieutenant.

"Manuel, the first job is to learn where we stand. That's up to you. Ride down there, locate the Texas brigade, find out its strength and how fast it's moving, then meet us at Raton. Only damn fools would go plowing in there blind."

The New Mexican saluted, not solemnly but gaily, laughing. "The chore is a gift, Colonel. I am homesick anyway." He winked at Price, got up and went out at an eager stride.

Jack Price told Slough, "They can't be in too bad shape down there if those people are joining up with us. We may have a chance."

"With the miners, sure we do. But Manuel's tribe is easygoing. They may sign up but when there's a fight I have my doubts. We'll see."

CHAPTER THIRTEEN

The descent to Denver was a wild, ragtag, half-drunk carnival, a column by twos, threes, fours keeping step to its own bawdy songs as it poured out of Central City, singing until the boys ran out of breath down the mountainside.

It looked anything but military and not reassuring to Price. There were no uniforms of course and the weaponry included every type long gun made from fifty-caliber buffalo rifles to smooth bore muskets, though every man wore a revolver at his belt and a bowie knife in a sheath on his hip.

Only a third were mounted, most of those equipped with sabers. Slough explained that under an earlier threat of Indian attack a cavalry company had been organized and all who could afford it had added the long blades to their arms.

Price had doubts that these green men would stand against a well-organized Confederate charge but after a first attempt he gave up trying to drill them. As boisterous as if they were on holiday, none of them would take orders from even their own subordinate officers, and, looking forward to a long, dry march, they had loaded their packs with Taos whiskey.

One thousand and forty-two miners of assorted origins.

By the end of the first day they were all roaring drunk. In the morning, cold and bleary-eyed, they were quieter, winding between snowbanks higher than the riders' heads. When they got down the grade and reached the plain they were out of whiskey, out of sorts, and tiring. J. D. Slough pushed them on. Jack Price's skepticism lessened a little when the volunteers knuckled under to the man they had elected, slogging on to the capital city.

He felt a tug of pride in them when they arrived, the way they shaped up and stepped out smartly to pass through streets lined with waving, cheering Denverites who made a parade route to the center of town and there the volunteers formed in ranks to be welcomed by the Governor with Chivington at his side.

Slough presented himself as their elected colonel, presented his officers and swore their allegiance to the Union. Gilpin made a small speech of gratitude, less than inspiring to the tired miners, then Chivington wanted a say.

He was a fiery orator with an evangelist's background, a hell-fire preacher who played a crowd expertly. With rolling, compelling words that thundered like drumbeats he exhorted the ranks for an hour to give their all, their lives if necessary for God, for Country, for their Homeland, for their Freedom, for the men and women who depended on them alone to save them from the Texans who were marching relentlessly up to kill and conquer.

Jack Price listened in bewildered astonishment. Was this the arrogant doubter who only three nights before had been so contemptuous of the threat he now shook in their faces like a scalp lock? What had made him change his mind? Or had he? Was it only exhibitionism to manipulate an audience for manipulation's sake? Whichever, it did not matter. He brought the weary company to a huzzah-ing rededication to the unequal challenge ahead. Finally he dispersed them to the saloons as if he were their commander.

Governor Gilpin was caught under the spell as much as anyone. Turning to follow the volunteers, Jack Price heard Gilpin tell Chivington, "Colonel, you could keep them inspired, add to their strength if you would go as their chaplain."

Price stayed, afraid that this strange colonel would wreck the unity of the miners if he attempted to pre-empt Slough's leadership, and his suspicion was confirmed by the man's answer.

Affronted, Chivington squared himself and announced, "Governor, I am a soldier first, a man of God afterward. If I go with that company I go to fight. At their head. My rank and experience make me their leader."

Price's hope sank. A captain could not protest to a colonel of his army. But Gilpin was not in the chain of command and proved his metal now.

Firmly he told the Colonel, "These are civilians, sir. Individualists. They elect who they will follow and they have not elected you. If you try to force your claim they will quite simply go back up the mountain."

Chivington flushed and the arrogance was back. "They're a rabble. They need professionalism. But so we don't lose them I will go as Lieutenant Colonel."

Jack Price held his breath until Gilpin shook his head, saying, "They have a Lieutenant Colonel, Manuel Chavez."

"A Mexican? Good God why?"

"He is familiar with the ground they will fight on." Gilpin was not giving an inch. "I cannot interfere. The First Colorado Volunteers are J. D. Slough's command. I can ask if he will brevet you at Major."

Chivington was stone faced, debating. Price read in the pause that the man was looking to the future. He could not afford to let this regiment march without him, leave a blot on his record, and at length he submitted with ill grace.

"I will speak to Slough myself."

He headed stiffly away toward the saloons in search of his new commander. Price looked at the Governor and found a bright amusement in his eyes but Gilpin did not mention his victory, reaching for Price's hand.

"A fine job, Captain. Don't discount your recruits, they'll come through better than you think. There is news here you can't have heard. Calhoun took his detail south the day after you left. I assume to meet with the Texans."

"That's a relief." Price smiled. "He didn't take Ann and Sue with him, I hope?"

The Governor laughed. "No indeed. He sent them to me after he had gone, escorted by Charlie Harrison just before Harrison left, and I moved them in with Miss Steelman's aunt. Miss Ryan was quite worried about you until I told her where you were and why." He noticed the color Price could not keep from rising in his cheeks and without mentioning it added, "I think they would be glad of a visit now that the ordeal of your joint captivity is behind you. There's no need for you to spend the day with your men. But come to my house for the night."

Gilpin gave him directions and Price rode the black across town to a building in a low area, built high off the ground because of frequent flooding.

Ann Ryan opened to his knock, a new girl from the tired, ragged, disheveled being he had last seen, wearing a new dress, her shining dark hair wrapped in a thick braid at the back of her head. Her eyes brightened and she reached for his hands.

"I'm so glad. Governor Gilpin said you were safe but as long as Calhoun was in town I worried. Did you find recruits?"

"Over a thousand." Her touch made his voice gruff. "Has there been any word of your father?"

"Not yet." Her chin lifted and she sobered. "It's a long walk from Sterling, moving only at night. Or they may have made it to the mountains." She held up a hand to stop further questions. "Wait until I get a wrap and we'll walk."

She brought a shawl. After the cold of Central City, Jack Price found Denver warm with approaching spring, but still there was a bite to the wind and the girl pulled the heavy crocheted triangle close as she left the high porch at his side.

On the sidewalk she told him, "You were about to ask about Sue, but her aunt could hear." Her tone turned dry. "She has the vapors because Virgil Calhoun was very attentive while we were kept at a hotel, then he left without telling her. Jack, she's not acting after all. She just doesn't care what he is besides a handsome gallant, but she's shrewd enough to hide what she feels from her Northern aunt. Mae Steelman would turn her out if she knew. Now what's your news? How long before you march?"

Walking with Ann Ryan on this bright morning, Jack Price wished he had more than this one day. He said sardonically, "Tomorrow, if we can pry the boys out of the saloons. The way they're celebrating I wonder what kind of soldiering they'll do when a fight comes."

"I'll bet on them. They're mountain boys and they play hard when they can, they work hard and they fight hard."

They spent the day walking aimlessly, a time Price would cherish. More and more he knew this was the girl he wanted to come back from the war to. If he came back. He left her for a moment before a store, bought a locket but did not give it to her until they were back at the house and it was time to go to Gilpin's, then pressed it into her hand and hurried away before she could refuse it. It could be the last time he would see her.

J. D. Slough and Colonel, now Major, Chivington were with the Governor looking like cats full of cream.

"Good news," Gilpin announced as soon as Price walked in. "We have reinforcements. Four hundred regular army troops with two batteries came in from Kansas today. That gives you over thirteen hundred men."

Jack Price did not bring up the comparison of this number with three thousand Texans should they meet the full force together. But that might not happen and it was encouraging to have regulars to bolster the volunteers.

They started south at dawn. Slough said it was near two

hundred and fifty miles to Raton Pass and he did not spend his men on a hard push. Still once they were away from the Denver bars the volunteers settled down and made almost fifty miles a day, so that a week after leaving Denver they climbed the grade of the pass that wound through the Sangre de Cristos and down into New Mexico.

By March 7 they had crossed it and camped for a needed rest while they waited for Manuel Chavez. This was wild, rugged, barren country, more desolate than any Price had seen, a dry and forbidding territory.

The New Mexican officer arrived on the twelfth with a wealth of information, little of it reassuring. As he had predicted the Southerners had come up out of Texas from El Paso following the east bank of the Rio Grande into New Mexico. High basaltic cliffs kept them on that side hunting a crossing. The two they reached first were ten miles apart, guarded by Fort Craig, where Union Colonel Canby was headquartered on the west bank just north of the brutal desert Jornado del Muerto, which the Texans would have to go through. Pandero crossing was south of the fort. Valverde north.

The Southern force was desperate for water, unable to get down to the river until they reached Pandero, and they far outnumbered Canby's garrison. Under General Sibley they tried the first crossing but were beaten back and had to go on to Valverde. There after a skirmish they forded the river, disdained to attack the garrison, by-passed it and continued up the west bank.

At Albuquerque Sibley's men occupied the town with no resistance, then took Santa Fe easily and were now resting in Las Vegas before coming on for Fort Union, just above Glorieta Pass in Apache Canyon. The fort was an important objective because it was the main supply point for all Federal troops in New Mexico. Manuel Chavez had heard Sibley had a thousand men.

When the Lieutenant Colonel had stopped at the fort, Major Paul, in command, had all his available men in skirmish positions at Glorieta but was so sure they could not hold that he had mined the fort.

Chivington went livid hearing that. On the march from Denver, Jack Price had discovered J. D. Slough to be not only a leader but a diplomat, asking Chivington's opinion and advice so that both men were now commanding the column.

Pounding a fist in his palm, Chivington raged, "If Paul blows that fort he leaves the whole territory at the mercy of the Texans. Chavez, how far is the pass? Can we beat them there and keep them out?"

Chavez spread his hands in doubt. "Some of us, I think. It's better than sixty miles."

Chivington swung on Slough, talking fast. "I'll take the cavalry. We can make it before morning. You bring the infantry and batteries as fast as you can. I need Chavez for guide."

"Go to it." Slough ran, shouting orders to start the foot soldiers on their way.

Price, still riding the black, was included in the cavalry and they rode immediately. South of Raton the country opened into high grassland that had once fed the great buffalo herds and was now becoming a rich beef-producing section, well watered, good for traveling.

The Captain was no stranger to forced marches but he had never ridden at the pace Chivington set through the night, stopping only briefly to let the heaving horses blow, then driving again, possessed by urgency. In less than twelve hours they were in the Fort Union stockade.

Haunted by Fort Sedgwick, Jack Price warned Chivington to be wary of a treachery here but the Major shrugged it off. If the Confederates had come Major Paul would have exploded his mines, and that had not been done. They rode under the Stars and Stripes as the early light shone on the 'dobe wall around the post, cheering that the buildings still stood. The skeleton garrison tumbled out in explosive welcome. Major Paul strode from his office to meet them, his face drawn from a sleepless night, his haggard eyes scanning the company in disappointment.

"Thank God you're here, sir," he told Chivington. "But we're still not strong enough to stop Sibley's troop."

"We'll stop him." The Major bawled it in his fire-eating voice. "There's infantry behind us on the double bringing two batteries. What's the latest on the Confederate position?"

"They stopped at the mouth of Apache Canyon on the tenth and are still there. Could be waiting for more men to come up."

"That gives us breathing time, then. Let's hope they stay there until our main force gets here. We'll rest here for them unless you get word the Texans are moving."

The upward of four hundred cavalry were dismounted,

billeted to sleep through the day and were roused in the evening by fresh shouts from the parade.

Slough's volunteers and the regulars dragged in after a sixty-four-mile march made in less than twenty-four hours.

All the officers combined a supper and a conference on strategy. Major Paul and Manuel Chavez with a knowledge of the locality advised that in the morning they should advance over Glorieta Pass and rendezvous at the Pigeon Ranch near the summit.

The ranch, Paul explained, belonged to Alex Valle, a Frenchman who loved dancing and had named his property for a violent step in the square dance called cutting the pigeon's wing, a heel-clicking leap.

No courier arrived during the night to warn of a Texan advance and at dawn Fort Union emptied, the column climbed the narrow, twisting trail to the ranch.

The March sun was warm, the craggy sides of the pass bright with cactus bloom and flowers that sent roots deep into the rock crevices for water. The ranch made a good headquarters with a built-in beef supply and proximity to the ground where a fight would develop. Valle was a volatile, exuberant host, drawing detailed maps of the local geography, describing where emplacements would be most effective. There could be no better place to engage the Southerners than what amounted to a trap at the top of Glorieta.

The Union force was well rested when information came that an advance guard of the Texans was starting up Apache Canyon. Slough and Chivington split the command, Slough posting half the infantry behind the natural rock fortifications beside the trail, Chivington concealing the cavalry behind a spur of hills below. Manuel Chavez held the rest of the miners across the narrow summit.

A long Texan line appeared, dragging field guns up the grade. Discovering the men above them, they opened fire, raking the canyon with grapeshot. The miners gave no ground, firing back to decoy the Texans closer. The defile roared with noise but little damage was done to the Union boys.

As the Southerners advanced the men in the rocks found the range and drove them back for a regrouping, but what they backed into was a flanking charge by Chivington's cavalry, yelling, flashing sabers, a surprise that routed Sibley's force in disarray.

They left behind thirty dead, forty wounded and above seventy taken prisoner.

Chavez's miners and Slough's foot soldiers poured down behind them in pursuit until Chivington blocked the way with the cavalry line, shouting above their victory yells to turn them back. Slough came before him waving his arms in angry protest, his strident voice high with excitement.

"What the hell, man, clear the trail. We got them on the run, let's get after them and finish them off."

Chivington sat his horse rigid in the swirling dust kicked up around him, and could be heard by everyone.

"Enough. Use your heads. It's after sundown. You'd run head on into their full force in the dark if you hauled our batteries down and you don't know what kind of firepower they've got or where it is. Go on back to the ranch for the night."

Chivington's cool reasoning was professional. He had fought fearlessly hand to hand, trampling Texans under his horse's hoofs, surprising Jack Price with a joyous fury in his attack, but immediately after the Texans ran he became a thinking machine, stopping the volunteers from a heedless rush into disaster.

Slough calmed down, got his men in hand, they gathered the prisoners and their own five dead and fourteen wounded and repaired to Alex Valle's Pigeon Ranch.

The following day scouts reported what looked to be the main Texas force moving into the lower canyon and the discovery of a ranch at the bottom where they were entrenched. Manuel Chavez knew it to be the Johnson spread.

"There's a back way in from here," he said. "It's a hard trail but we can get behind the Rebs before they know it, tonight."

Slough was delighted, saying he would keep the foot soldiers to hold the pass, that Chivington and the cavalry should go with Chavez and make a surprise raid. All day they waited at the crest of Glorieta but the Southerners did not appear. At evening Chivington's four hundred riders followed Manuel Chavez over a roundabout course of remote, dangerous trails through brutal mountains that brought them at noon the next day to the rim of a line of almost sheer cliffs. Below them lay the Johnson Ranch, where the Confederate supply base was established, and what they looked down on was impressive in its extent.

Chavez guided them single file down a narrow, steep, treacherous path where the horses slipped, slid, stumbled into each other, in peril of falling off the edge at every step, but they made the bottom safely, undiscovered by the garrison of some two hundred men. Hitting it in a wave when the Rebels had no idea there was an enemy within miles, they drove the Texans out in a swift route. Then systematically they destroyed the supply trains, ammunition carriers, an artillery piece and the Confederate livestock of over seven hundred mules. Behind them they left a blaze of more than sixty wagons. Afterward they made the hard climb back up the cliffs and returned to the Pigeon.

There was bad news, bewilderment and a miracle to be told there. While the cavalry was away Slough had taken his volunteers toward the pass and been surprised by a heavy contingent of Texans almost at the crest of Glorieta. The unexpected meeting with Southern horsemen in such numbers panicked the miners who had fought so willingly in the first encounter and they beat a hurried retreat across the pass.

It was a clear victory for the Texans and if they had chased the men on foot they would have ridden them down and had no further hindrance between them and Fort Union, no barrier to Denver. They had not. Instead they had turned about and taken themselves down canyon the way they had come. Why?

Chivington, Chavez, Price and the cavalry had the answer. There must have been a desperate race from the Johnson Ranch with a report of the ruin of everything there. They were denied the material for moving and fighting, in a harsh country of hostile people, and their position was impossible to maintain.

Sibley's column would have to fall back until they could reoutfit. To Santa Fe at least.

CHAPTER FOURTEEN

J. D. Slough's volunteers had done a lot of walking in a very short time, with fighting at the end of it. They were young and strong, but when Chivington wanted to chase the retreating Southerners immediately Slough vetoed him. Chivington argued that the rebels were easy prey, reeling from the loss of their ammunition, food stock and transport. Slough did not deny the fact, but his men needed rest and they too were low on supplies. The Texans, he said with Manuel Chavez's backing, could not find enough material to do them any good short of Santa Fe, which was another long march that should not be required of his tired company. Neither could the Rebels move faster than infantry with many wounded to carry and artillery pieces to drag with them. They could be caught up with later. Slough's decision was to retire to Fort Union, rest men and animals, care for their own wounded, and restock from the stores there.

They left the Pigeon Ranch with beeves requisitioned from Valle and spent three days at the fort. On the fourth they were ready for the trail but before dawn an excited sentry reported a company of mounted men approaching from the south.

Appalled that Texans could have so quickly found the

means for a new advance and were north of Glorieta pass, Slough and Chivington threw everyone to man the stockade. They waited in the dim light, making out a small body of men whom they outnumbered probably four to one. That was the first relief.

The column halted at a distance and a standard-bearer rode in. As he closed the early light showed the flag to be the Stars and Stripes, which Jack Price cautioned might be a ruse to put them off guard, but the man was permitted to come before the gate. The announcement he shouted up was the last thing the garrison expected.

Colonel Canby was arriving from Fort Craig with his militia.

The officers inside went down to the parade but left the men above until they could be sure this was the truth. The gate was opened and shortly the Commander in Chief of the Federal troops in New Mexico led his force in.

Canby was of medium build, his hair dark, a full beard concealing his mouth and lower face. He acknowledged the salutes then dismounted, showing exhaustion as he swung down, beating with his gauntlets at the red and yellow dust covering his uniform. It was so thick on his face that his eyes seemed to peer through holes in a mask.

He shook hands with the officers in dispirited silence. He was the only one of the new arrivals wearing blue, less than fifty men altogether.

As he took the offered hand Chivington asked, "Where is the rest of your force, sir?"

Canby waved listlessly at the thin rank. "All that's left are here."

Chivington was incredulous. "Out of two thousand? Where did you lose that many?"

"Later. Let me dismount these and will you billet them."

Major Paul gave the order to his sergeants, then trailed the Commander and officers to the big orderly room. Canby sank heavily into a chair.

"Now to your question. We were outnumbered at Craig when the Texas brigade came through. They drove us back to the fort. After that my men quit, just melted away. Haven't the Southerners been here yet?"

Chivington reported on the Glorieta action, acidly stressing that Slough had lost the pass in his hurried retreat and that when disaster had been prevented by the raid on the Johnson Ranch he would not take his command after the routed Texans.

"It's surprising you didn't run into the retreat on your way here."

"We nearly did, though we didn't recognize what it was. Our scouts spotted dust of a large column in time that we could avoid it, pass around it. There were too many of them for us to meet." He slumped deeper in the chair, his eyes closing, his chest sinking in a long exhalation.

Price said quietly to Major Paul, "Shouldn't you offer him a bed? He must have ridden all night."

The Major was young enough to have overlooked the marks of weariness on the Commander. He started with a guilty glance at Price, offered his own quarters and when Canby accepted escorted him to the room. Slough threw

Chivington a sour glare and took himself away. The conference was over for the time being.

Late in the day when Canby had slept, washed and his orderly had done what he could about the sweated, dusty uniform, the officers were called together again. Canby was more remote, more the military chief than he had been under the morning's distress. He sat stiffly and his voice was sharp.

"Mr. Slough, without Major Chivington the Texas brigade would have taken this fort, then taken Denver. Their way was cleared when you abandoned the pass, you ran before you lost a man. Therefore I will entertain your resignation."

Slough crimsoned, saying hotly, "We were on foot and they all had horses, sabers. They'd have wiped us out. And, sir, in this country the volunteers elect their officers . . ."

Canby cut him off, biting out, "They are nevertheless under me for the duration of this campaign. I mean to use them to drive Sibley's force back out of New Mexico and I must have aggressive officers at their head. Chivington will take the command. I brevet him Lieutenant Colonel with Manuel Chavez as his deputy. You are relieved."

It was a harsh blow to J. D. Slough and Jack Price thought it unfair. The man and his miners had fought fiercely in the earlier engagements, but it was true they had panicked at a crucial time and place. Slough's outthrust jaw indicated that he would try to pull his volunteers out, take them back to the mines. Price wondered if they would follow him that far and thought not. They had had a taste of war and showed an appetite for more even after their rout, unlike the men who had disappeared from Canby at Fort Craig. The room was silent as Slough lingered, then stalked out.

Canby switched briskly to the business of a pursuit of the Southerners, asked Paul for a map, spread it on the table and traced a trail.

"I believe they will return by the way they came, down the Rio Grande rather than tackle the more rugged Santa Rosa Pass out of Albuquerque or other mountainous paths. They will have found some material at Santa Fe but not sufficient for another attack here. Major Paul, Colonel Chivington, between us the regulars, the First Colorado men and what can be spared from this garrison will give us the strength to run Sibley back to Texas. If you will muster them out I will talk to them myself."

"Before that, sir, I have a report that can be important in the pursuit."

Jack Price waited for Canby's permission and once more detailed his discoveries of who was wrecking the Overland stations, of the guerrilla band presumably now with the Texans and possibly still wearing blue uniforms that would deceive the unwary, thirty-four men at his last count. Canby had a full vocabulary of barrack-room damnations and exhausted it on the Southerners and all of them felt better for it when they went to review the troops.

While the ranks were falling in the stockade gate was opened again and Alex Valle herded in another jag of beeves that Paul had sent for when Canby's party had turned up. Excitable as he was he reacted to the sight of the expanded force with a high laugh and swung his horse to the side of the officers, his mouth stretched to a wide white grin.

"Ah. The Colorado war is won and everyone rides back north?"

Chivington introduced the Frenchman and Canby, adding, "Everyone rides south to keep pressure on the Texans' retreat."

Valle lifted his shoulders, spread his palms in confusion. "So? But the detail that was on their heels turned back. They were going north when they stopped at the Pigeon. Why was that?"

"What detail? Everybody who was at Glorieta is here."

The rancher trotted down the line of cavalry, then back, perplexed. "I do not see them. I would recognize the Captain with the especially fine face. They came through last evening needing food and water, then passed on."

Jack Price choked, his mouth suddenly dry. "Did he give his name?"

Valle shrugged. "Not to me."

"Did you get a good look at him? Can you describe him?"

"A very good look when I took them all to the cook shack to be fed. He is fair, tall, very gallant in his manner, but he has a lieutenant who frightened me. Reeves he called him."

"Calhoun. How many with him?"

"They were twenty-one all told. Is something wrong?"

"Wrong enough. They're Southern raiders in stolen uniforms. They've lost a number or maybe they split up." Price swung to Canby. "Sir, they're headed back to the

Overland route and they can play havoc with the line. Let me go after them. With luck I can find them at Denver, but if they pass there before I make it there's no guessing where they'll go and General Curtis' force is spread much too thin to protect the stations."

Canby swore another string of oaths, drawing a whistle of admiration from the rancher. "Yes. I wanted all the cavalry with me but this man has to be stopped. Take twenty, whoever you choose."

"The miners, sir. They know the area and man for man they're as good fighters as I've seen. We'll leave as soon as we can load pack horses."

"Good hunting and good-by. I pray you find them."

Price saluted, broke away and ran toward J. D. Slough, mounted and in bad humor at the end of the rank, took his bridle and led him out of earshot to tell him the mission, ask him to engage the best volunteers he had and commandeer the strongest horses while Price was having the pack animals made ready with rations and ammunition.

Slough came alive in an instant. He was out from under Canby and Chivington and the manhunt was a challenge he jumped at. In half an hour he had picked his people, had them at the gate, all eager for the new sport. Moments later Price brought two heavy-chested pack animals and they lined out toward Raton.

It had taken a week to make the march south over this ground when it was imperative to reach Apache Pass before the Texas brigade. The Union had won there and in these few days the whole balance of power in the territory had been reversed. Now, not burdened with infantry or batteries, they could make better time, perhaps even overhaul Virgil Calhoun before he got to Denver since he had passed Fort Union only the night before and had less than twenty-four hours' head start.

Price pushed his detail until midnight and camped at the foot of Raton Pass, not putting the animals up the grade after the seventy-mile drive. But at first light they began the climb.

Slough had chosen both animals and men well. The horses moved strongly and fast for long periods and the miners rode singing, happy to be off to a war of their own with their chosen leader and the Captain they had adopted, happy to be heading for their familiar stamping ground.

That night they stopped north of old Fort Pueblo and the next halfway between the Springs and Cherry Creek. But they had seen no sign of Calhoun, no campfire ahead, so he too must have ridden hard.

Anxious as Price was to come up with the Southerners before they passed through Denver and vanished in the empty land along the Overland trail, he had to weigh the condition of his detail against the possibility of an extended search. It would be foolhardy to rush in with tired animals and men, against an enemy Price must respect. Taking the guerrillas would be hard work at the least.

The audacity of the men, hundreds of miles from support, riding back into the capital now that they had been unmasked, proved a dedication among them that would be hard to match in the Union Army. The Federal forces were riddled with draftees whose will to fight was questionable.

Many were Europeans fresh off the ships with no background, no roots in the nation, men who were paid to enlist by Americans who chose not to serve in the ranks.

The Southerners' emotions were ingrained deep. Loyalty to their cause made them fine soldiers from their general officers down to the simplest infantryman. They commanded Jack Price's admiration of their abilities even though he did not agree with their aims, and he had no illusion that they would not fight bitterly. Calhoun's band was equal in number to the handful of miners and if Price could not stop them their raiding would go on in their determination to cut the west off from the east.

With Denver nearly in sight Price had to rest his men and mounts in order that they be fresh when they entered the town. He could only hope Calhoun would be there, that he would find them at the Criterion Saloon headquarters. But haste could bring defeat so he pulled to a halt half a day short of the capital.

Slough was impatient, bent on making amends for the retreat at Glorieta, urging Price to let him ride on alone.

"I can go in and find out what the situation is, then come back and meet you so you'll know what's up there."

"Good. But don't come back. Report to the Governor. You make a swing through the camps for more recruits if you can find any. If we have to chase Calhoun on north I'd like to make two details and cover more territory in a shorter time. Tell Gilpin we'll come in after dark tomorrow night."

Slough rode, not pushing his horse too hard, but man

and animal would have had about all they could take at the end of the trail.

Price watched him leave then went to the cooking fire and poured himself coffee, wishing there was whiskey to lace it and quicken a relief from his aching tiredness.

CHAPTER FIFTEEN

It was dark under an overcast sky when Jack Price rode up alone to Gilpin's rear door and announced himself to the sentry there. He was expected and admitted, the guard escorting him to the study, where the Governor waited. Gilpin greeted him warmly, shaking hands, pouring brandy as the sentry returned to his post.

When the man had gone Gilpin lifted his glass in a toast. "To the boys who turned the Texans back. That's the best news I've heard all year. Slough told me some of it when he came to leave word for you, but he was in a hurry to get off to Central City."

Price drank with him before he asked, "What did he find out for us here?" The liquor was welcome warmth after the chill ride.

"Nothing more than what I knew, but you're here in time. Calhoun rode in as bold as brass and is still around."

"Nobody challenged him? He's being left alone?"

Gilpin's smile was wry. "His status is not generally known. As nervous as the town is blue uniforms look encouraging whoever wears them, and if the Indians attack the Southerners will help fight. Anyway, there are so many of them in the home guard they're too strong to move against. I'm very glad you're here, but what about Slough? Why did he leave his command?"

So the miner had not admitted he had lost it. Price saw no gain in telling Gilpin at this time. It would be learned later, hopefully after Slough had blotted over the record by a success with Price.

"Canby took over," he said. "When we found Calhoun was coming back it was decided Slough was more valuable here, where he can recruit more help to stop the raiding. About Calhoun, is he openly going in and out of the Criterion in blue? Isn't it known as a Southern hangout? Wouldn't he betray himself?"

"They use the back entrance when nobody's looking. Where are your people?"

"Coming in one and two at a time. We'll meet on Holladay Street behind the saloon at midnight, stay out of sight and try to pick up the Copperheads as they come and go. With luck we should be able to arrest most of them without giving an alarm and avoid a fight that we might lose."

"Tonight?" Gilpin was startled. "You're not waiting for Slough's reinforcements?"

"We shouldn't need them here with Calhoun still around. I wanted them in case we had to chase him up the trail where he'd be hard to find." Price looked at the Governor's tall grandfather clock, the hands reading ten minutes until twelve, and excused himself.

Gilpin saw him out the back way and Price left his horse in the yard to walk through the dark streets.

Even the red lights of the district were turned out, the

pleasure houses shuttered against a storming by the tribes. Price's miners were slipping in behind the corner saloon on foot, their horses left picketed at the edges of town. They had come from different directions to avoid suspicion of a group passing the home guard patrols that probably contained Southerners. Price found them scattered in deep pockets of shadows, moving from one to another to ask if any had been challenged. All except one had slipped through without being seen and that one laughed softly.

"I ran into a bunch that wanted to know what I was doing breaking the curfew. I said I was from Central City and my mother down here was sick and had sent for me. It worked. One of them had been up there and seen me a couple of months ago."

They were positioned along the alley where anyone coming out through the rear door would have to pass close to them, their guns ready to be jammed in backs and sides. Silent, they waited two hours, the cold night penetrating their clothes. The door had not been opened once. Price gathered them together to change the strategy, choosing two to reconnoiter inside.

"I want to know how many are in there and what they're doing. Claim you're home guard and cold and need a drink. I thought that before now they'd be heading for the warehouse they slept in when they came to town, but if they look as though they're going to stay here until daylight we'll have to go in after them before then."

The two delegates went around toward the front entrance and the rest continued waiting, moving about more than they had, restless and, Price suspected, wishing they were the ones chosen to get out of the cold for a moment and fortify themselves with whiskey. It must be torture to these volunteers who were more used to indulging themselves than following uncomfortable orders, yet no one complained. Price was proud to have them with him and confident they would fight well if it came to that.

He was beginning to be concerned that the two inside had been recognized as Northerners and were being held. He warned the detail to be alert for a surprise and raised his rifle to the ready in the crook of his arm. Footsteps echoed on the walk. They could be Southerners who had pried information of the ambush out of his pair. Price sent a whisper along the line behind him. Then a low call came around the corner.

"It's us, Rick and Ben."

The volunteers appeared, stopping before Price when he spoke, Ben reporting flatly, "There's thirty Rebs in there. Most in blue, the rest in town clothes. Five playing poker, a lot at the bar drinking, everybody else rolled up in blankets on the floor at the back."

"Damn." Price did not like the added number. "Sounds as if they mean to spend the night." He debated pulling back, waiting another day, taking the risk that Calhoun would ride out in the morning and complicate capturing him.

While he considered the delegate Rick laughed softly, saying in an airy tone, "So say the word, Captain, and we'll go haul them out."

A murmur of approval went through the group and Price felt a warm admiration for these men who had seen the Rebels' ability at Glorieta and were still willing, even eager to face them again, even outnumbered.

"Good. Good." Price joined the ripple of quiet laughter. "Let's figure how we do it."

He spelled out a plan of action. Four men to stay in the alley to drive any Confederates back who tried to come out through the door there. Price would take the rest to the front. There four others would go in on the same pretext the first two had used if they were questioned. They would buy drinks and when they were served one would stroll to the poker table and watch the game, three would be ready to cover the bar. Price would watch through the front door until all four were positioned, then he would lead a rush with the remaining twelve and all would throw down on the room.

Fifteenth Street was black and silent as they eased along the side of the Criterion. Larimer was empty when they reached that corner and turned it. The curfew was serving them well. Price lined his dozen along the front wall of the saloon, where they could pivot in quickly after him. The four advance men opened the door and walked in, not having to fake the shiver as warmth touched their cold bodies. The last one closed the door but Price held it open a crack to see through.

He saw Calhoun at the bar watch the newcomers with suspicion that faded somewhat when they paid no attention to anyone, rubbing their hands briskly, rifles tucked under their arms as they came against the counter, but his hand dropped to the butt of his revolver and he challenged them.

"Who are you?"

The man nearest him showed surprise. "Home guard of course. Who else is out at night?"

"Two others were here ten minutes ago. What are you loitering around this place for?"

"Taking turns. We can't all be off the street at once and we've got to thaw out once in a while. Anything wrong with buying a drink?"

Calhoun spoke over his shoulder to Harrison. "Ever see any of these before, Charlie? Are they all right?"

The saloon owner was unsure. "I don't know them. They must be new in town and don't know where they are." He did not say aloud that if they were familiar with Denver they would surely react to seeing Union uniforms in the Criterion. "There are a lot of strangers coming in to keep away from Indians. I wouldn't worry." The words were slurred, thick with liquor.

Calhoun was still edgy, saying sharply, "All right, have a drink and clear out. This is a private party."

He sipped his own drink, watchful as the four were served, then as one picked up his glass and started toward the poker table his voice cut the air.

"No. Have your drink and go."

The volunteer looked at Calhoun's hard eyes in confusion, slowly tipped the glass against his lips and let his rifle drop into his hand, aimed at the floor.

"Hell, man, where's the hurt in . . . ?"

Charlie Harrison shot him through the throat.

Jack Price cursed, yanked the door wide and plunged into the room with the twelve on his heels, each spreading to the side, guns up. The three at the bar covered their area. Price's rush and shouted order pulled the Southerners' attention from its momentary concern with the crumpling body.

"Hands in the air empty, everybody."

They spun, gaping at the bristle of barrels pointing at them and sweeping over them. Many hands were raised, Calhoun's lifting very slowly as he faced the rage in Jack Price's face. Charlie Harrison was drunk but not so drunk as to draw the gun he had just slipped back to the holster. For a moment there was no movement from the stunned Rebels.

Two more shots exploded in the second of silence. The two big lamps hanging from the ceiling shattered. Price had a glimpse of the man behind the bar, crouched and only his head showing, a smoking shotgun nosing above the counter in front of him. Then the long room was blacked out and a tumult erupted.

Men rushed toward both doors seeing nothing, bumping into each other trying to get out before fire started. There was a volley of blind firing from the volunteers at the front wall toward the rear beyond where they had last seen the three at the bar, but that stopped quickly when Price shouted. In the scramble for the doors neither side could tell where its allies were, neither dared shoot, and a grim silence fell as the deep sawdust on the floor muffled the running boots. There was only rasping breathing.

The front door was pulled open, the front windows crashed out. The dim glow of a recently risen moon showed dark figures jumping through the openings but

Price could not tell whether they were his men or Calhoun's. He stayed where he was midway of the room until even the breathing was gone except his own, and the place felt emptied, then, sweeping his rifle before him to locate obstacles, he groped toward the lighter oblong of the front door, bent double to present a smaller target.

There was a short gun battle in the street where there was light enough to identify uniforms. A Southern voice cried, "I'm hit, damn it, I'm hit." Boots ran on the sidewalk across the road. Price reached the door, looked around the jamb, did not see movement and slipped out, kept low and sprinted for the corner. Bullets tracked him, slapped against the brick wall behind him but he was not hit and ducked into the cross street.

There had been shooting in the alley too but that had stopped before he left the saloon. The moon did not touch the building here and Price paused to listen for further action. There was none. The engagement on Larimer had broken off. The attack had been a waste and Calhoun, if he had survived, was warned. Price walked on toward the alley and was challenged by a voice he knew, one of the volunteers.

He said quickly, "It's Price. What's the story here?"

"Pretty fair. We thought we'd lost you though."

"Too dark for good aim. Who did you lose?"

The man laughed. "They're lousy shots, Captain. We took a few scratches, nothing serious, and we got the first five Rebs when they started boiling out the back, then they slammed the door and didn't try again. Everybody's here but Tim, who they say caught it inside. What do we do next?"

"Some thinking, first."

Price's major worry was that Virgil Calhoun would ride out now, and if the guerrillas got clear of Denver he saw the devil's own time finding them again. There was no guessing what direction they would take and since the towns and ranches were all abandoned there would be no one to see them pass. It could take weeks, even months to run them to earth and he knew he could not hold the volunteers that long. Spring was in the air and the minute the mountains were free of frost they would rush back to the mines.

He must stop Calhoun here or nowhere. There was one more chance. Only a few roads led out of Denver and if he could cover those with a volunteer at each the Southerners should be spotted on their way out. Whoever saw them could alert the rest of the detail and it could take Calhoun's trail before he lost himself in the wide territory.

When Price explained he drew a doubt from a redheaded boy who laughed.

"If I was them I'd be gone already. They're sure not around here anymore."

"I don't think so, Jeb. They didn't intend leaving tonight and I doubt they're prepared. They'd be heading into country stripped of food, guns, and ammunition. It will take some time to load what they'll need. Go watch the roads and one of you mousehole their warehouse. The rest of us will look to the gunshops and stores they're probably breaking into. Let's find them."

He detailed how they should spread themselves. Jeb would go to collect their horses to be able to communicate more quickly if Calhoun appeared. Jack Price and the remainder would each walk a semicircle, half in one direction, half in the opposite, spreading from the saloon outward along the streets. These would meet at designated corners as each circle was completed. In effect they would cast a net over the whole town and sooner or later, Price felt, someone would come upon the Southerners.

It was nearing four o'clock by the time everyone knew his route or position and those of the others, and the late moon was high, washing the streets with translucent silver. They would have to use caution to dodge home guard patrols should any still be roaming the city, though at this time of night Price doubted any were. It was the hours before midnight when men were tempted to break the curfew.

When they separated Price took the perimeter of one half-circle, moving from block to block. As he ranged farther from the center of the search and turned back on another lap the men between him and the Criterion, having covered their first course, would then retrace his way one at a time so that the area would be looked at more than once, should the guerrillas be indoors and missed on a single passage.

Price saw nothing, heard nothing on his first tour. He met his opposite number at the agreed place, moved outward another street and turned back paralleling the way he had come. Neither he nor the next man he met had had any luck. He wondered if Virgil Calhoun had gone to ground, would keep out of sight all night and the next day to wait out a search he was shrewd enough to expect, anticipating that the volunteers would be sure by the following night that he had escaped.

He was halfway to his next man when a horse whinnied, another echoed it, muffled sounds coming from the Knox livery midway of the block.

The noise drove him into a shadowed doorway to look closely at the street ahead. It was empty. Across the road the big two-story frame barn was a visible bulk with no near neighbors. A mere suggestion of lantern light made the oblong of the doorway a shade different color than the moonlit street.

Jack Price slipped back the way he had come until he knew he could not see movement in front of the building should there be any, nor be seen, then crossed over to the empty lot beside the corral, turned into that and warily, careful that his feet did not kick a can or bottle or discarded box, followed the corral fence.

It was long, dipping down at the back to Cherry Creek and into the water so animals inside could drink from the running stream. There were horses there, perhaps two dozen, but Price could see none saddled. Climbing through the rails and moving slowly, silently so the animals would not take fright and begin milling, he threaded through them until he could look into the rear of the runway and saw what he had hoped to see.

The lighted lantern was well toward the back. Its glow showed a team hitched to a wagon, headed toward the street. Men in blue uniforms were there loading grain

sacks and baled hay. Standing at one side was Virgil
Calhoun with Charles Harrison at his shoulder, Harrison
too now wearing blue.

Price could have used his rifle, shot the pair of them and
taken his chances of getting away from the others, but that
would be plain murder and all his instincts and training
rose to refuse that option. Instead he eased back through
the corral, crossed the lot to the street, then ran, his boots
quiet in the deep dust.

Racing then, unable to reach his next contact without
passing the front of the livery, he went searching for the
volunteer who was following him. It took time to find him.
He had not yet reached the meeting place and Price went
on, growing short of breath but pushing his pace until a
figure called a low, guarded, "Captain?" from an alley
mouth.

Gasping, hurrying the words, Price got out, "Calhoun's
crowd loading at Knox livery. Go send the word around to
the boys." He liked the grunted triumphant laugh, the
speed as the messenger whirled away, and sagged against
the wall to fill his lungs.

CHAPTER SIXTEEN

The moon was down and the first hint of light heralded the March morning by the time the volunteers had come together again. Jack Price described the barn and corral for those of the mountain boys who did not know it. They could circle it, attack from the rear, cut the Southerners off from their horses and charge the runway, drive Calhoun's men back and into the open street. A part of his group would be posted at the front corners of the building to catch the retreat.

It was a simple strategy and even though the numbers were uneven surprise and confusion should equal the odds. But again it went awry. From a long block away Price saw the wagon, now on the street across from the livery, in front of a shop where a lamp burned. Two men were carrying a heavy box through the door. Calhoun's detail was divided. But Price's men at the front could handle those from the shop. He gave explicit orders. No firing until those all came out. They should be shot then and that would be the signal for the rear attack.

Price led everyone along the creek bank to the corral, sent four ahead to the far side of the livery to move to the front, the bulk of the men to wait in the corral and took three with him along the near wall to that corner.

From there he could look across into the shop, where a carved wooden rifle hanging over the door identified it. Inside the lamp shone on Calhoun, Harrison and two bearers just bringing out a second ammunition crate. Sight of them lifting the box into the wagon ruined the surprise. A volunteer on the other corner also watching found temptation too great. His rifle exploded twice. The bearers were thrown back and down, the ammunition dropped.

Raging with frustration, Price saw Calhoun and Harrison spin to the shop door, drawing, but before they reached it a fusillade from the back of the barn thundered through the runway and a man beside him cut loose toward the shop.

Price could read the two Southerners' minds in the way their heads swiveled toward his corner, then the other. They were bracketed and knew it. They could not cross the street to join those in the livery without committing suicide. They stood hesitant a second, then Harrison caught Calhoun's arm, jerked him off balance and dragged him stumbling toward the rear of the gunshop, where there must be another door.

Price could not follow them, could only know they were lost to him again, for men in blue were erupting from the runway into the street, firing into the barn as they ran, and he had his work cut out stopping them, driving them back inside to face the guns there. Four of them dropped in the dusty street, then the rest were out of sight in the barn to take their stand in whatever shelter the box stalls would give them.

Shots still sounded, hollow in the confine of the building, but most of the firing came cracking from the corral. The volunteers were in control and Price breathed easier. The Southerners bottled up inside would soon have to make their choice of falling or surrender. He was not concerned with them. It was Calhoun he wanted and now there was time to go after him. Calhoun was the leader and if he were not caught there were enough Rebels in Denver and the mountains that he could recruit another band and go raiding the Overland again.

Angling across the road, Price ran for the gunshop and surprisingly bullets whipped after him. Someone in the livery was still watching the front. Weaving, he made the door and dodged through, running the length of the store toward an open window at the back. He nosed his rifle out first, edging his head forward until he could see the alley. The early light showed a row of wooden buildings across the narrow strip of dirt. Calhoun could be in any of them or even out of the area, making still another search necessary, and Price would need men for that. The immediate order of duty was to finish the livery fight. He ran toward the street again.

Halfway there he stopped short. A uniformed figure had stepped into the livery entrance, where he could not be seen by the volunteers at the corners but could look across into the lighted shop. The way he stood, arrogant, defiant, told Price it was the Southern Lieutenant Reeves, the instinctive killer.

Reeves had a rifle at his shoulder and before Price could bring his up it fired. The bullet brushed close to Price's head. He broke the frozen second, dropped to a crouch, steadying his gun against his side and sent his shot across as Reeves fired again. Price knew he had scored in time to deflect Reeves's aim a trifle, enough that Reeves's shot missed.

Reeves staggered, then recklessly strode forward, continuing to shoot, getting off two more bullets before Price, stunned by the relentless advance, shot again and saw the man's face explode in red. Even then Reeves managed one more step, but that leg collapsed and he pitched forward, the rifle still at his shoulder until he sprawled on the ground.

Price's breath hissed in and out. He had been under fire many times but never faced one man such as this, whose determination to kill him seemed extended even after death.

Still crouched, Price turned to shoot out the lamp and waited where he was for minutes. There was daylight in the street now but the shop was still dim with shadow and there could be other guerrillas watching for a sight of him. Belatedly it came to him that he had heard no other firing since Reeves had fallen and as he watched another man in uniform appeared in the runway, a white cloth tied to the end of his rifle, waving it up and down where the men at the corners could see it.

The Southerners were surrendering. Cut off from Calhoun, Price thought they would have given up before if Reeves had permitted it. Or, since these were men who made a profession of deceit this might be a ruse to bring him into the open where he could be murdered.

From behind the doorjamb he called across, "Come for-

ward with your hands over your head." He did not want
that rifle with the white rag on the barrel going off when
he stepped out.

The man walked uncertainly to the center of the street,
the rifle held high in one hand. He wore a uniform with the
hash marks of a Fort Sedgwick sergeant, whether or not
that was his real rank with the Confederates. Price went to
meet him, noting that the eyes were wide and dark with
fear.

The voice was unsteady, asking, "What terms, Captain?"

Jack Price's face was hard. He need not make any terms
with people who rode posing as Indians, who killed civilians, who wore stolen uniforms. They did not deserve military justice. But if he denied them they would hold the livery until the last was killed. They had nothing to lose by
that and it could cost Price further casualties than he had
sustained. His own tone shook with his anger.

"What do you want?"

"To be treated as prisoners of war."

"How many of you are there now?"

A disbelief changed the Sergeant's face. "Only eighteen,
sir. We lost half the boys last night."

"The sympathizers who were with you in the Criterion,
they're not here?"

"No. They all hightailed after you broke in."

Price figured rapidly. Eighteen Southerners as a nucleus
and the town swarming with men who would befriend
them. Where could they be held secure without the danger
of breakout? Nowhere in Denver certainly. The surest

thing would be to hang them, but, professional as he was, the idea galled him.

He said flatly, "Tell the detail to leave their arms and come out one at a time, hands over their heads."

"The terms, sir. Do I have your word we have prisoner-of-war protection?"

"You do. But only to prevent more bloodshed."

The Sergeant dropped his rifle at his feet, turned and called the order loudly and the men in blue filed out. Price also raised his voice to bring the volunteers. The prisoners looked defeated but relieved that they were not to be handled as the renegades they were. In contrast the miners came whooping their victory, encircling the guerrillas, who stood in a cluster supporting the several wounded. Price took the Sergeant aside.

"I've kept my word. Now pay for the lenience you don't deserve. Where would Calhoun go from here?"

The man's jaw thrust out in sudden defiance. "He's a fine officer, sir. I can't betray him."

Price leveled a finger under his nose. "He's an outlaw killer. Shall I change my mind and hang you all? The Colorado Volunteers would enjoy such a show. It's your choice, that or tell me Calhoun's plans."

The Sergeant's face lost color. He looked toward the men under the miners' rifles and dropped his shoulders, said barely audibly, "To take the girls we brought from Sedgwick as hostages to get you off his back. Said he'd kill the dark one if he has to."

It was like a body blow to Jack Price. He had trusted Calhoun's upbringing to keep Ann Ryan safe from violence. Now it appeared the brutality of his raiding had corroded him, turned him craven. He caught the Sergeant's arm and roughed him through the volunteers into the circle, then stalked to the towhead Len Sliter, whom he had delegated his lieutenant, speaking rapidly.

"Take over here. I have to hurry. Get these Rebels to Fort Morgan and tell the commandant to guard them close until I can come. Tell him why. If any of them try to break on the way shoot them."

"Glad to, Captain. How do we pass them through the road patrol?"

"Go to Gilpin, have him escort you."

Price ran. There might not be time to saddle a horse. Calhoun and Harrison had been gone from the gunshop long enough to have reached Mae Steelman's house already if they had headed straight there, but Price counted on their having not. They would need a rig or at least horses for the kidnap. But intercepting them could be close. The thought of missing them chilled him through.

A picture in his mind gave him strength and speed, of a sleigh before the house, of the girls being wrestled or carried out to it calling for help. He ran to the street and saw ahead no such picture. The house was closed. There were no sounds from it, no rig out front. If he was too late there would be lights, the aunt waked by the struggle to take Ann Ryan even if Sue Steelman had gone willingly; there would be hysterics from Mae Steelman.

There was none of this. Price stopped at the walk, his chest pounding. He must wake the girls, spirit them away, but to charge in like a whirlwind would only frighten everyone and cost precious minutes. He stood gasping, calming himself, and was still too distraught to knock at the door when the jangle of harness reached his ears.

Spinning toward the sound, he saw a sleigh turn the corner drawn by a pair of prancing black horses, fresh and wanting the run. Price ran again, heavily, toward the porch and around it, stopped there and drew his short gun. The rifle he had abandoned when he started here so its weight would not slow him. Out of sight he watched the sleigh draw up, saw Harrison drop out and go to hold the heads of the dancing team, saw Calhoun drop the reins then, jump to the ground and stride up the walk.

Price stepped sideways into view, the gun raised, called sharply, "Here, Calhoun. Hands high."

The Southern Captain flung toward him in a crouch. For an instant he did not move, then his hands moved up slowly. But his eyes warned Price. When the right hand was less than shoulder high it spit flame from a holdout derringer snapped out of the sleeve. The little bullets clipped past Price as he twisted aside. Then his own gun exploded, once and again.

Calhoun grabbed at his throat, jarred back and fell. In his concentration on this enemy Jack Price had for the moment ignored the other. He swung toward the saloon man now, firing again, missing, just in time to take Harrison's bullet in his side.

The heavy slug spoiled Price's second shot. It went high, hit nothing. He saw that as he fell, then was stunned when his head cracked against the hard ground. His mind still reeled as Harrison left the team, stepped forward and put two more bullets into Price's back.

Veering to Calhoun, Harrison needed only a glance to know the guerrilla leader was dead, his throat blown apart. The Southerner turned his attention to the horses the gunfire had spooked. They had bolted, straddled a tree down the block, overturned the sleigh. Harrison walked to them deliberately. It was not in him to be afraid. He righted the sleigh, untangled the harness, made sure the animals were sound, backed them clear of the tree and without looking behind him climbed to the seat and headed south toward Raton and New Mexico beyond. Denver would never see him again.

In her bedroom upstairs Ann Ryan came out of sleep, jerked awake by the shots. Disoriented by the sudden awakening, she sat a moment, then threw back the covers and ran to the window. She saw Calhoun's sprawled body on the walk just beyond the porch roof. The roof hid Price at the corner of the house. Harrison and the sleigh were out of sight further down the block. Wheeling, she snatched the robe from the bedpost, flinging it around her just as the door slammed open and Sue Steelman ran in belting her robe, her blue eyes wide, crying sharply.

"The shots. So close. What is it?"

Ann Ryan did not tell her, only pointed to the open window and followed the girl to keep her from falling out when she saw the man on the walk. Virgil Calhoun's hat lay at one side and his face was upturned. Sue Steelman leaned over the sill, her hands white clutching it, for a long moment. Then she shrieked. She did not faint but, still shrieking, flew out of the room toward the stairs.

In the hall Sue collided with her aunt, just coming from her room, sprang away from her and continued her flight, hardly touching the treads as she ran down them.

Ann Ryan came into the hall more slowly, was stopped by Mae Steelman catching her arm and throwing hurried questions.

"In the front yard. We'll have to go to her."

Throwing off the hand, Ann Ryan took the steps down three at a jump. Even so when she came out to the porch Sue was already sitting splay-legged on the walk, Calhoun's bloody head in her lap, rocking and continuing to scream. Ann ran toward her off the porch, meaning to slap the blond girl as hard as she could to stop the hysteria, but the corner of her eye saw a second figure on the ground. Looking that way she discovered Jack Price. Harrison's two bullets in the back had had the impact to turn him on his side. Ann saw the contortion of his face, knew that he was not dead yet, ran to him and dropped to her knees, calling his name through a choked throat.

He was conscious, opened his eyes and tried to smile but pain warped it. He whispered, "It's over, Ann," but could say no more.

Mae Steelman came from the house, her head swinging from one girl to the other, Sue in her loud lament, Ann gently investigating the red stain on Price's side, then those on his back. Neighbors were gathering, hanging back, little more than curious in this land that lived so intimately with violence. Jack Price was vaguely aware of murmurs above him, then Mae Steelman's voice, strident with command, making him wince so that fresh pain burned through him.

"You, Willie Stevens. Quit your gawking. Run and fetch Doc Petrey on the double."

Sue Steelman kept up her high, throbbing wail that pierced Price's ears like a knife. He frowned, groaned, wishing the ugly sound would stop. Then Ann Ryan's cool fingers were on his forehead, massaging lightly the wrinkled brow. A moment later they were taken away. Something smooth, warm, hard was pressed against his lips and Ann's breath touched his cheek.

"This is your locket, Captain. I wear it day and night. Hold on. It isn't over for us. Get well. Get well."

He smiled again, fumbled blindly for her hand, held it and felt her strength flow into him through it. He lay quiet and she did not move.

Mae Steelman's voice again, jarring the dangerous peace Price was sinking into. "Here, girl, scissors and cloth. Cut that shirt and stuff the holes, stop what bleeding you can. I have to get that hysteric niece inside, then I'll make up a bed. Have Doc bring him."

The movement of his shirt against his body felt like sandpaper scrubbing away Price's skin. Then like a hot sword a wad of cloth was forced into the crawling flesh of a wound. Jack Price passed out. He did not feel the probe when Petrey pried Harrison's lead slugs out of his flesh.

On and off through blackness he would swim up to half consciousness, hear voices but not words, feel a touch, then nothing again. But Ann Ryan's locket was chained around his neck and in those periods of near lucidity his fingers would close around it.

The half-wakeful moments became more frequent, lasted longer. Price held onto life, fought for it with his unconscious mind. At last a voice came clear, a man's, objective.

"Fever's down this morning. How's the twitching?"

Next, Ann's soft, steady tone. "That stopped in the night, early. He slept quietly."

Price's eyelids flickered but were too heavy to open. He tried but his body would not respond and took him down to sleep again.

It was one more morning when his lids lifted and held wide. He rolled his head, saw the bright, empty room and knew a panic that he was abandoned. He filled his lungs and shouted. Footsteps ran in the hall outside. The door was flung inward and Ann came through in a rush to the bedside. She saw his open, clear eyes on her, saw him relax and laughed suddenly, clapped her hands once and held them together.

"I win. I told him."

Price raised his brows, too weak to move anything more. Ann's sudden, radiant smile made her beautiful.

"Doc Petrey, I bet him you'd pull through. He said no. You'll be starved. You haven't had a thing but the little broth we poured into you for a week. I'll bring . . ."

She didn't finish, leaving at her long stride, and was soon back with a bowl of thicker soup. She lifted his shoulders, packed pillows behind him and spoon-fed him while she talked.

"There's good news for you. Your Len Sliter was a good choice to manage the guerrillas. He was most methodical, kept the prisoners cooped in the livery all day while he rested the volunteers in relays. He thought it was foolhardy for tired men to try to travel that stretch to Fort Morgan in daylight when nobody knew where the Indians were. That night he made a caravan with wagons for the wounded and trail supplies.

"But that's not the best. Father and Sergeant Lynch came back."

Price shifted higher, feeling stronger to hear of something finally going right, asking, "They're in town and in good shape?"

"In good shape, yes, but not in town. Two hours before your detail was to leave Slough came down from the mountains with ten more miners. Father and Lynch came with them. They had walked to Central City from Sterling, gotten there two weeks earlier, but they were so worn out and had lost so much weight they didn't try to come on. When Slough came up they were ready to move again and Father joined the volunteers. Sergeant Lynch came along in a dither to get back to an army unit. So they all went with Governor Gilpin leading them out of town like a Fourth-of-July parade."

She fell silent but there was a mischief dancing in her eyes that nothing she had said accounted for. Watching her, Price felt a smile grow around his mouth, stretching his stiff, drawn face almost painfully, and he guessed.

"There's more. Something good about poor Sue?"

Ann shrugged that away, sobering. "Sue's in collapse.

And disgrace. Governor Gilpin told Father where I was and he and Lynch came to see me. Lynch let the cat out of the bag to Sue's aunt, who the handsome Yankee Captain Sue was crying over really was. Mae Steelman is no ninny to take that kind of defection lying down. She has Sue locked in her room and says she'll keep her there for the duration of the war or until her niece agrees to nurse at a hospital where the Union wounded are."

The mischief came back, brightening the girl's whole face. "There is something more, though. Something for you. The Governor sent a message with Len Sliter to be wired from Fort Morgan to Washington. They got an answer and a courier rode all night. Gilpin himself brought it to me last evening. On your report of our escape from Julesburg Sergeant Lynch is made an officer. And you . . ." She broke off, set the soup bowl on the floor, wedged her hands behind his neck. Price thought he was about to be kissed but she was not ready for that yet. She straightened back holding the slender gold link chain he had worn all week. "I'll take back my locket now, Major Jack Price."

Todhunter Ballard was born in Cleveland, Ohio. He graduated with a Bachelor's degree from Wilmington College in Ohio, having majored in mechanical engineering. His early years were spent working as an engineer before he began writing fiction for the magazine market. As W. T. Ballard he was one of the regular contributors to *Black Mask Magazine* along with Dashiell Hammett and Erle Stanley Gardner. Although Ballard published his first Western story in *Cowboy Stories* in 1936, the same year he married Phoebe Dwiggins, it wasn't until *Two-Edged Vengeance* (1951) that he produced his first Western novel. Ballard later claimed that Phoebe, following their marriage, had co-written most of his fiction with him, and perhaps this explains, in part, his memorable female characters. Ballard's Golden Age as a Western author came in the 1950s and extended to the early 1970s. *Incident at Sun Mountain* (1952), *West of Quarantine* (1953), and *High Iron* (1953) are among his finest early historical titles, published by Houghton Mifflin. After numerous traditional Westerns for various publishers, Ballard returned to the historical novel in *Gold in California!* (1965) which earned him a Golden Spur Award from the Western Writers of America. It is a story set during the Gold Rush era of the 'Forty-Niners. However, an even more panoramic view of that same era is to be found in Ballard's *magnum opus, The Californian* (1971), with its contrasts between the *Californios* and the emigrant gold-seekers, and the building of a freight line to compete with Wells Fargo. It was in his historical fiction that Ballard made full use of his background in engineering combined with exhaustive historical research. However, these novels are also character-driven, gripping a reader from first page to last with their inherent drama and the spirit of adventure so true of those times.

I